RETIREMENT WAS MURDER

An Amy Bell Mystery

David Schwinger

ISBN: 154405534X
ISBN 13: 9781544055343
Library of Congress Control Number: 2017903483
CreateSpace Independent Publishing Platform
North Charleston, South Carolina

Also by David Schwinger

The Teacher's Pet Murders
Murder Spoils the Perfect Romance
Murder with Magic
Murder Takes the Top Prize
Murder on the Lido Deck
Letter-Perfect Murder
Willing to Murder

To all the wonderful residents of our active adult community here in Florida.
If some residents think they recognize themselves in this book, they are mistaken!

Saturday
January 31, 2015

Max Gattner had spent nearly an hour walking around the cavernous social hall at the clubhouse, and that was just about all he could take. It was the community's annual club event. Residents wore their ID tags, newer residents introduced themselves and mingled with the other residents, and the various clubs had tables set up to showcase their activities and recruit additional members. There were also pitchers of free beer and sangria, as well as soft drinks.

Max had made small talk with lots of residents—most of whom he found quite distasteful. Finally, he had stopped at the desk of the Yankees/Mets Club, of which he was a member. In an hour and a quarter, after the club event would be over, the YMC was going to meet in club room B and view a film about the 2000 World Series, when the Yanks had defeated the Mets.

The two men at the YMC desk were wearing the official club jackets with both Yankees and Mets logos on them. Because of the coming meeting and film, Max was wearing his too. He told the men at the desk that because of the sangria, he was feeling a bit dizzy, and he was heading over to the club room to relax and await the movie. Actually, he did feel a little tired, but that was also a good excuse to get out of there.

Twenty-five minutes later, relaxing in one of the well-cushioned chairs in club room B, Max glanced at a magazine and smiled as he contemplated the stupidity of most of the members of the YMC. (*Come to think of it*, Max decided, *most of the non-YMC-members in the community are just as stupid!*) Just last week, he had won a twenty-dollar bet with Richard Garmin. Richard had insisted that in the sixth game of the 1986 World Series, the Mets had trailed Boston by two runs, but then they scored three runs in the bottom of the ninth to win the game. Max had bet Richard that he was wrong. Actually, the Mets had scored the three runs in the bottom of the tenth, so Richard had to pay up. Max decided, with great satisfaction, that it served that jerk right. Richard was an Obama-hating racist as well as a Yankee fan.

The box containing the new baseball caps had just been delivered to the club room, and it was sitting next to Max's chair. The caps had been a special order. Half of them had a Yankees logo on the front, and the others had a Mets logo. All had the stylized letters SDE (for "South Desert Estates") on the back. Max took one of the Mets caps out of the box and put it on.

No one else had yet arrived for the movie, which was still fifty minutes from starting. Max put down the magazine he had been looking at and closed his eyes. He had consumed numerous alcoholic beverages at the social hall, so maybe a brief nap would be a good idea. That way, he'd be alert for the film, despite the fact that—unlike 1986—the 2000 World Series did not have a happy ending for his beloved Mets.

Less than two minutes after Max commenced his nap, someone quietly entered the club room and picked up a souvenir bat signed by Yogi Berra from a table in the back. The visitor came up behind Max's chair and bashed him repeatedly on his cap-covered head. The visitor then exited the club room, unobserved.

About twenty minutes later, several YMC members arrived at the club room for the movie. They found Max's dead body. The movie was postponed to a later date.

***

Over the weeks that followed, the sheriff's office interviewed many residents of the South Desert Estates active adult community. Their investigation was going nowhere, a fact which did not displease a large number of residents of the community. But when a New York City private detective came to visit, several residents requested her assistance in solving the case. This was very bad luck for the killer.

Saturday, March 7, 2015

"**W**ill you please wipe that disgusted look off your face? This is going to be fun!"

Amy Bell was speaking to her husband, Jeremy Green, while they were enjoying a take-home dinner consisting of a large pepperoni pizza with several additional toppings.

Amy had been expounding for several minutes regarding their coming two-week vacation to Arizona, during which time they would be celebrating her parents' forty-fifth wedding anniversary. Actually, while Amy referred to it as a vacation, Jeremy referred to it as a trip.

"Sweetheart, maybe I would be a little more enthusiastic if I didn't have to 'look forward to' your parents—and sometimes even your brothers—repeatedly harassing me about my political views. Did you have to tell them that I admire Ronald Reagan?"

"Jerry, you know I told you that it just slipped out. I'm sorry." Amy smiled as she stroked her husband's cheek. "But you always hold your own with them."

Jeremy was quite sure that it didn't "just slip out" and that his wife wasn't sorry. He was, in fact, correct. Amy's parents were progressive liberals who had successfully transferred those political views to their daughter and their two sons. In fall of 2009, shortly after

Amy and Jeremy became engaged, they flew to Phoenix to visit Amy's parents, who had sold their hardware store and retired. In December 2008, they had moved from Queens, New York, to the South Desert Estates active adult community—where at least one owner and one resident of each home must be age fifty-five or older—located several miles southeast of Arizona's capital city. Amy, with a giant smile on her face, had introduced Jeremy to her parents with the words, "Mom, Dad, this is my fiancé Jeremy—and he loves Ronald Reagan!" She had made the same kind of introduction of Jeremy to her older brothers, who had both moved to Phoenix several years prior to Amy's parents' retirement.

Amy enjoyed nothing more than watching her family sock it to her husband regarding his politics. It was her way of getting back at Jeremy, who, while not as political as his wife, loved to bait her with nasty comments about Barack Obama's policies. Amy always answered back in kind, but she knew that she—unlike her parents—had to maintain civility and good humor with Jeremy.

Amy never forgot that her political views had almost ended her relationship with Jeremy before it even started, when Amy was twenty-two and Jeremy was three years older. On a Friday evening in March 2007, Amy and her best friend, Cathy, were sitting at a table at Marty's, an East Side Manhattan singles' bar, when Jeremy and his friend Eddie came over and joined them. Eddie was interested in Cathy. Amy and Jeremy went upstairs to a quieter table for two. Things were going great until Amy asked Jeremy who he admired and he said Reagan. Amy immediately launched into a tirade of insults, which became louder as Jeremy tried to defend himself. Then Amy said she was going downstairs to get her coat.

Amy had actually found Jeremy very interesting and sexy. At five feet eleven, he was seven inches taller than Amy. He had classical good looks. She was going to ask Jeremy to come back with her to the apartment she shared with Cathy. But Jeremy understandably assumed that Amy's actions indicated that she hated him—and that she was a nutcase to boot. He left Marty's and went home. When Amy, Cathy, and Eddie went upstairs to get Jeremy, they discovered he was gone.

Luckily, Eddie—who really liked Cathy and eventually married her—convinced Jeremy to phone Amy the next day and give her another chance. What ensued was a torrid affair of several months' duration. But they were young and unrealistic, and they decided to date other people. They became friends with benefits for two and a half years, at which point they realized they had loved each other all along.

They owned and resided in a two-bedroom, two-bath co-op apartment in Greenwich Village. Amy was vice president for sensitive investigations at Spy4U Services, and her husband was a freelance consulting actuary who usually worked from home. Amy always told her parents (as well as everyone else) that marrying Jeremy was the best thing that ever happened to her and that he was everything to her. But whenever she and Jeremy visited her parents (usually once or twice a year, as a stopover on the way to another destination), her dad took her aside and asked her how she could live, day after day, with a fascist. At times, she thought he might be serious.

"Remember, Jerry, we'll be with my family for only four nights."

Her husband moaned. He had hoped it would be for only two nights, the typical time period for these visits. But because of the big anniversary celebration, he had been apprehensive all along that there would be a more extended visit.

Amy continued. "Then we'll do some sightseeing. We can visit Lake Powell, the Petrified Forest, the Grand Canyon, and some other places too. And, of course, as usual, we'll stay at a hotel on the days we're seeing my family. My parents keep saying they want to put us up in their house. Of course, I can't tell them the truth, which is that at any time, I might act on an uncontrollable urge to rip off your clothes and conquer you right on the living room rug." Amy licked her lips and smiled at her husband, while continuing to stroke his cheek.

At this point, Jeremy was no longer thinking about the trip. He reached inside Amy's pants and grabbed her rear end. "The rug, eh? But you're wrong about who's gonna conquer who!"

The pizza remained half-eaten as the couple proceeded directly to the living room rug.

A few minutes after they finally returned to their pizza dinner, the phone rang.

"Amy," the caller announced, "this is Susan Blackstone. I'm the chairperson of the activities committee here at South Desert Estates." Amy turned on the speakerphone. "Your father and mother, Irving and Carole, will be celebrating their forty-fifth anniversary, and I understand that you and your husband will be visiting here to join them in their celebration."

"Yes, Susan, you are correct. We will be coming."

"Well, Irving has, for years, been telling everyone that his daughter is the top private detective in New York and that you have solved some very tough cases, including several murders."

"I am indeed a private detective, but my father is understandably going to exaggerate my talents."

"Amy, I did some checking on the Web. Irving is pretty much correct. On behalf of the activities committee, I am inviting you to give a presentation in our social hall. You can speak about your background, your job, and some interesting cases you have solved. When will you be here?"

"We plan to arrive on March nineteenth and leave on the twenty-third. My parents' anniversary events will be on the twenty-first and twenty-second. But no one would be interested—"

"You're too modest," Susan interrupted. "Everyone will be very interested. In fact, I expect it to be the most exciting—and best-attended—presentation of the season! I spoke to Irving and Carole, and they are so proud that you'll be speaking. We'll schedule it for Friday evening, March twentieth, from seven thirty to eight thirty. That way, it won't interfere with your parents' anniversary activities. You'll speak, and then there can be questions from the audience. There will also be free coffee, soft drinks, and desserts available, provided by the committee. The doors will open at seven. This is going to be fantastic!"

Amy knew she was trapped. "Can my husband, Jeremy, say a few words too, as part of my presentation?"

"Sure, that would be icing on the cake! I'll send you a confirming email with all the details. We're all so looking forward to seeing and hearing from you."

Amy hung up. She was not pleased. But Jeremy knew just the right words to say.

"Will you please wipe that disgusted look off your face? This is going to be fun!"

Thursday, March 19, 2015

Amy and Jeremy took United's nonstop morning flight from Newark to Phoenix and landed at Sky Harbor airport before ten in the morning. They rented a car and drove to the Mesa Suites Hotel in the town of South Desert, where they checked in for a four-night stay. At one o'clock, after eating lunch at the hotel, they headed toward South Desert Estates.

Irving and Carole Bell had inherited their hardware store from Irving's father. The business never made a great deal of money, and they had always thought they could never afford to retire. But the land the store was on, which they had also inherited, ended up being much more valuable than they had imagined. The money they received from selling the property and their home made it possible for them to retire and relocate to Arizona. Their new home, which had cost them so little, in comparison to prices in Queens, had over two thousand air-conditioned square feet, including two bedrooms, a den, a breakfast nook, and a dining room. There was also a two-car garage. Everything was on one level.

As always, Amy and Jeremy were greatly impressed by the lavishly decorated entrance to the community, with its large, welcoming arch. They had to stop at the guardhouse to gain access through the gate. The guard on duty recognized Amy and Jeremy from past visits and gave Amy a pass for five days. They proceeded to Tall Cactus Lane, a well-named street as large cacti were in abundance in the beautifully landscaped areas in front of each of the houses. The monthly fees paid by the residents to the community association were partially used for this landscaping. Amy pulled into the driveway for house number 13424. They got out and rang the front doorbell.

Carole Bell opened the door and hugged and kissed her daughter for fifteen seconds. Then she shook Jeremy's hand and invited the visitors in. After being greeted by Irving, Amy and Jeremy joined her parents in the living room for wine. After a few perfunctory questions to Amy about how things were going, Irving got down to business.

He turned to Jeremy. "So, Mr. Reagan-lover, who is your choice for the Republicans to nominate for president next year?"

"Well, Irving," responded Jeremy in a calm, soft voice, "I think my first choice would be Governor Walker of Wisconsin. I hope he decides to run. He had the tenacity to stand up to violence, and he won his case with the people of his state."

"Are you crazy?" Irving was already raising his voice. "Walker is the biggest union-buster in the country. He hates working people. Actually, I'm not surprised you support him. You and Walker care only about making the rich richer."

Jeremy remained calm. "Actually, Walker's policies are creating more good jobs and greatly aiding the Wisconsin economy."

Now Carole chimed in. "Actually, I hope Walker is not nominated. He manages to fool people into voting for him. He's a slimy reactionary, but he's a good politician. I hope the Republicans pick Donald Trump. He quit his TV show, so he's probably going to run. And he would be a sure loser in the election."

Irving seconded his wife. "You bet! But the Republicans—stupid as they are—are not stupid enough to nominate a pompous egomaniac like Trump, whose biggest accomplishment is repeatedly saying, 'You're fired'!"

Jeremy glanced at his wife, who had her hand over the lower part of her face, clearly trying to hide the fact that she was laughing. He had a decision to make: Should he or shouldn't he?

He decided he should. "Trump's biggest accomplishment is a real-estate career of more than forty years in New York City, creating jobs and revitalizing neighborhoods. He helped save New York City by building in Manhattan during the tough times in the late seventies and early eighties. He understands how to negotiate and make deals. He's not my first choice for president, but I like him a lot."

"You can't be serious!" Now Irving was screaming. "Trump is a spoiled rich boy who only cares about getting richer. If he ever got elected—which, of course, couldn't possibly ever happen—he'd turn the whole population into indentured servants, forced to work to increase his wealth."

Jeremy smiled at Irving and lowered his voice even more than before. "Am I correct in inferring that you probably wouldn't vote for Trump or Walker?"

At this point, Amy could no longer control herself; she burst into hysterical laughter, which stopped the other three in their tracks. It took twenty seconds before she calmed down. Then she spoke. "Mom, Dad, you know you're not going to get Jerry to change his mind. I want an update from you two about what's going on here at South Desert Estates."

Amy's parents got the message and did not continue the debate. They discussed their recent activities in the community. Amy then inquired about her brothers, Simon and Jacob. Nine and eleven years older than she, respectively, both were married and each had two children. Carole gave Amy the latest gossip and also provided the details regarding their forty-fifth anniversary dinner. Just for close family, it would be held at a restaurant on Saturday. On Sunday, they had planned a big anniversary event for their friends and relatives at a local hotel, with dinner and dancing.

Then she changed the subject. "Amy, I want you to know how proud and excited we are about your presentation tomorrow evening. Do you know what you're going to say?"

Amy nodded. "I've composed some notes, and I basically know what I'm gonna say. Jerry will also say a few words. Then I understand I will be taking questions from the audience. And there will be drinks and dessert too. Jerry, are you ready to get up there and speak?"

Her husband smiled. "I know exactly what I'm going to say—and I'm not telling."

Everyone laughed.

Friday, March 20, 2015

There were forty tables for ten in the social hall at the South Desert Estates clubhouse, and they were all filled. The sign-up sheet had been full and closed for several days. Nearly one-fifth of the entire population of the community was there, either for Amy Bell's presentation or for the free drinks and desserts—or both.

At seven thirty, Susan Blackstone stepped up to the podium on the stage and introduced Amy, who began by thanking the activities committee for inviting her to speak. Then she congratulated her parents on the occasion of their forty-fifth anniversary. She spoke about her childhood in Queens and gave a humorous anecdote about her older brothers. Then Amy got to the meat of the presentation.

"I want to tell you about the two people who, apart from my parents, had the greatest effects on my life—and they were fantastically positive effects, thank goodness.

"The first person is Mr. Chester Murray, the owner and president of Spy4U Services, a New York City detective agency. In August 2003, I had completed my first year at City College. I was a political science major, and my goal was to become a lawyer. At that time, I needed a part-time job to help me continue my studies. I heard from a neighbor that there was an opening at Spy4U, and I raced right over to apply in person. I didn't even have a résumé, but Mr. Murray somehow saw the potential in me. He hired me on the spot.

When I graduated college, he offered me a full-time job, which I accepted. He has mentored me throughout my time at Spy4U, and has promoted me to vice president. He has done everything possible to facilitate my professional growth. And no, I do not have any more interest in going to law school."

At this point, Amy discussed some of the difficult cases she had solved, including two murder cases. Then she smiled broadly.

"The second person who had a great effect on my life is sitting right here in this hall, at the front table near the window. He is my husband, Jeremy. Before I married Jerry—that's what I call him—I was a manic, intolerant bully who was prone to yelling at people. Now, married to Jerry, I'm still sometimes a bit of a bully." She paused for laughter from the audience. "But I am, in general, a very happy, well-adjusted, tolerant person. Jerry is everything to me. And there's more. Jerry's an actuary; he's so smart! He helps me analyze my tough cases. There have been several cases I'm certain I never would have solved without his help. I have asked Jerry to come up and say a few words. Come on up, Jerry."

Amy walked over and sat in a chair on the stage a few feet away from the podium. Jeremy rose and walked up to the stage. As he kissed his wife and then approached the podium, a lady in the audience yelled out, "What a hunk! Do you lend him out?"

Another lady yelled out, "I want him first!"

It took about thirty seconds before the audience calmed down and Jeremy could begin to speak.

"Amy is not correct when she says I'm the smart one in the marriage. She has solved many cases where the police were completely clueless. Amy has insights that no one else has; she sees connections between events that no one else would see. There have been several occasions when I would say something I think is totally unimportant, and she would respond by telling me I just solved her case. Of course, I have no idea what she's talking about until she explains it to me. I will happily take credit for solving those cases, but I know that in reality, it's all Amy. However, the one thing I can legitimately take credit for is being the luckiest guy in the world."

Amy rose, and Jeremy walked over and hugged her for several seconds. While they were hugging, Susan Blackstone announced that Amy would now accept questions from the audience. Jeremy took the seat on stage, and Amy went back to the podium while members of the audience who had questions lined up.

There turned out to be a total of seven questioners. The first six asked about various aspects of the detective business, such as how Amy determines if someone is telling the truth and whether she has rejected some clients and why. Amy responded to these questions at some length. The final question came at twenty-five past eight.

"Hello, Amy, my name is Mel Barton. I'm the current president of the Yankees/Mets Club. Most of us in the club are from New York, like you. On January 31 of this year, one of our members, Max Gattner, was murdered in this clubhouse. The sheriff has made no progress, as far as we are aware. We need you to try to solve this murder. Will you please help us?"

A great rumbling erupted in the audience.

"Don't get her involved in this," someone shouted.

Another person yelled, "Yes! Please help us."

Amy was totally stunned. Speechless, she looked toward Susan for help, who came back on stage and went to the podium.

"Thank you, Amy, for your wonderful presentation. And thanks to all of you for attending." Susan escorted Amy and Jeremy off the stage and out of the social hall, while the audience was still in turmoil.

At eight forty-five, six people gathered in the clubhouse office of the South Desert Estates board of directors: Amy, Jeremy, Amy's parents, Susan, and Susan's husband, Ralph Blackstone. Ralph had locked the office door.

Susan spoke. "Amy, I want to apologize for what happened. Your presentation was amazing, and it was totally unacceptable for anyone to try to involve you in what happened to Max."

Amy looked at Jeremy, and he knew why. He shrugged his shoulders. Amy took this as permission. "Susan, can you tell me how Max was killed?"

"I'll let my husband, Ralph, give you some details. He is the president of the board of directors and also a member of the Yankees/Mets Club. He was probably the last person to see Max alive—other than the killer, of course."

"Wow!" exclaimed Amy. "You run the activities committee, and Ralph runs the board of directors? You two are quite the power couple!"

"Actually," Susan explained, "the rule in the bylaws states that whoever is elected president of the board of directors—it's by vote of the entire community—gets to select the chairperson of the activities committee. And the candidates for board president usually announce their choice for activities chair in advance of the election. So they kind of run as a team, and they serve for a term of one year. The previous board president, Darren Harwood, also selected his wife as activities chair."

Amy was confused. "Why would they have such a rule?"

Ralph chimed in. "The rule was in place when we moved here four years ago. We asked why, but we never received a decent answer. There must have been some kind of reason for it, originally.

"Anyhow, on January 31, a box of specially ordered baseball caps—having an insignia on the back of the cap with the initials of our community—was delivered to the clubhouse for the Yankees/Mets Club. There were Yankee caps and Mets caps. I am a YMC member, and I took out a Mets cap, put it on, and brought the box to club room B, where the YMC was going to be meeting and showing a movie at four o'clock. I got to the club room between five and ten past three. Max was the only one there; we greeted each other, and I put the box down next to where he was sitting. Then I went back to the social hall, where they were having a big recruiting event for our various clubs.

"When some other YMC members showed up at the club room at around three thirty, they found Max. He was dead in the same chair he was sitting in when I left him. His head had been bashed in. I got there a few minutes later. The murder weapon was lying nearby; it was the club's souvenir bat, autographed by Yogi Berra. I should add that when I brought in the box of baseball caps, I had observed the bat in its regular place, on a table in the back of the room. The authorities found no fingerprints on the bat. They interviewed tons of residents, but they basically have made no progress."

Amy asked the obvious question. "Did Max have enemies in the community?"

Susan laughed briefly and then stopped herself. "Amy, I'm sorry; I know this isn't funny. But nearly everyone here who knew Max disliked him. However, Irving, am I wrong in saying you were his best friend in the community?"

Amy's father nodded. "I was his best friend; actually, Carole and I may have been his only friends."

Now Amy was totally confused. "Dad, why didn't you ever tell me your friend was murdered?"

Carole responded. "Amy, your father and I would like to talk privately to you and Jeremy about this situation. Susan, Ralph, I'm sure you'll understand." The Blackstones nodded.

Amy also nodded. "Mom, Dad, let's go back to your home now."

Back at 13424 Tall Cactus Lane, Irving Bell answered his daughter's question. "Amy, I wanted to ask you to help solve the murder, but your mother and I were worried that you would be angry and feel it was an imposition and that you might also be afraid to visit us in the future, what with this murder hanging over the community."

Amy hugged her father. "Don't ever think like that. I love you and Mom; I don't want you to ever be afraid to tell me anything. Jerry and I were planning visit the Grand Canyon and a bunch of other tourist sights after we left Phoenix on Monday. If I take the case, we probably won't get to do much touring, so I'll need Jerry's permission. And I positively have to be back in New York on April second. In any case, you have to understand that I probably won't be able to dig up anything useful."

"Jeremy," Irving volunteered, "I can get you a pass so that, as my guest, you can play anytime on our tennis courts. And if you agree to let Amy investigate Max's murder, Carole and I promise never to argue politics with you again. And yes, Amy, we know it's likely your investigation will not hit pay dirt, but at least we can say we tried."

Jeremy smiled broadly at his father-in-law. "Irving, I'll take you up on playing tennis, but regarding politics, I wouldn't want to spoil all your fun." The other three laughed as he continued. "If your good friend was murdered and Amy can help, I'm not gonna stand in the way. But at this point, I think Amy and I should head for our hotel. We can all use a good night's sleep."

Amy agreed; she and her husband proceeded out the front door and to their car.

Back in their hotel room, Amy smiled at her husband. "See? I had good reason to originally be disgusted about being recruited to make the presentation."

Jeremy was contemplative. "Actually, the result of your presentation was that Irving opened up about his desire for you to investigate his friend's murder. Otherwise he would probably not have told you his feelings. So, I vote for your presentation having been a good thing."

Amy stared at husband as she ran her fingers through her long, black hair. "Jerry, that's incredibly smart! And you know how turned on I get when you say something smart like that. So, we're not getting any kind of good night's sleep until you completely satisfy me!" She unzipped her husband's pants and adroitly ensured that he would be totally focused on the job at hand. "And Jerry," she said, smiling and licking her lips, "I am never, ever lending you out!"

Saturday, March 21, 2015, a.m.

As Amy drove from the hotel to South Desert Estates, she contemplated some things she hadn't mentioned in her presentation.

She thought about the period when she and Jeremy were friends with benefits. Even though she was also seeing other guys, she had been very upset and jealous over the idea that Jeremy might be truly happy with another woman. She was, at times, an emotional basket case. It had taken two and a half years for them to realize they were meant to be with each other. Marriage had freed her, emotionally as well as sexually. She could be her totally uninhibited self with Jeremy, including physically. She knew how to make sure her husband was completely satisfied. She also knew how lucky she was.

At ten in the morning, Amy parked her car in the driveway of a house on Sunflower Drive. When the door opened, she was greeted by Mel Barton. Earlier, she had spoken to Mel on the phone. "Thank you so much, Amy, for deciding to look into Max's killing. I know I had no right to disrupt yesterday's meeting by asking."

"I agree," said Amy. "You shouldn't have asked—but I'm glad you did. Of course, you must understand that I have to be back at work on April second, and in any case, the odds do not favor me being able to discover anything new."

"Of course, Amy. We all know this is a long shot, but we're so grateful to you for trying."

Mel's wife, Annette, said hello and announced that she was going out to play volleyball. Mel led Amy to the living room. They sat down, and she accepted a Diet Coke. "So, Mel, can you please give me all the details you know regarding the events of January 31?"

"Okay, they were having the annual club event in the social hall, from one to three forty-five. All the clubs set up and man desks, with information and sign-up sheets. The new residents of our community come to check out the clubs and mingle with the other community residents, many of whom come to meet the new residents and drink some beer and sangria, as well as peruse the club desks. As president of the YMC, I—along with club VP Mike Whelan—manned the club desk.

"I had previously sent out an email to all the YMC members. First, I reminded them that at four o'clock, the club would be meeting in club room B to watch a forty-minute film on the 2000 World Series, and—"

Amy interrupted. "Is that the one where the Yanks played the Mets?"

"Yep, that's the one. So, in addition to reminding them about the film, I requested that all club members put on their YMC jackets and mingle with the community residents in the social hall during the club event. I felt that this would draw attention to our club and give us the best chance to recruit some new members."

"Mel," Amy interjected, "wouldn't the club members be kind of warm wearing their jackets?"

"Actually, the jackets are pretty light, and the social hall and club rooms are usually a bit too cool. People often wear jackets or sweaters there. Anyhow, at about two forty-five, Max approached our desk. He told us he drank too much sangria and was feeling dizzy. He said he was going to club room B to sit down and relax until the movie started. He said if anyone asked, we should tell them where he went. Then I saw him heading toward the exit.

"At about three thirty, I told Mike that I was leaving the desk and going to the club room to get things ready for the movie. Mike agreed to hold the fort alone for the final fifteen minutes. In the hall, on the way to the club room, I was joined by two other YMC members, Mark Oswald and Danny Kasden. We entered the club room and discovered Max's dead body in one of the chairs. His head was all bloody. A bloody Mets cap, with special lettering on the back, was on the floor next to the chair. Clearly, Max had been wearing it when someone battered him on the head, and it had fallen off.

"Also next to the chair was a box of the special baseball caps the club had previously ordered. We later found out that Ralph Blackstone had, just a few minutes earlier, brought this box into the club room. Ralph said he brought in the box at between five and ten minutes after three, and at that time, Max was in the same chair, alone and alive. Ralph said he put the box down next to Max's chair and immediately left. Max obviously had taken a cap out of the box and put it on his head before he was killed.

"We also found the club's souvenir bat, with Yogi Berra's signature, lying near the body. The bat was bloody; it was obviously the murder weapon."

Amy had a question. "Prior to finding the body, did you tell anyone what Max had told you about him going to the club room because he felt dizzy?"

Mel shook his head. "No. Nobody asked me about Max, and I told no one what he had said. Mike has stated that he also told no one. And I—as well as the sheriff's people—have spoken to all the other club members who were there that day, and they all say Max never told them he was going to the club room early. Some people said they observed Max mingling in the social hall. A few said hello to him. All those people said they saw him prior to two forty-five or could not say when they saw him."

"Did all the club members actually follow your suggestion and wear the club jackets?"

"Yes. There are twenty-eight dues-paying club members, and twenty-five showed up for the movie—of course, it was postponed. Darren Harwood was in the hospital, recovering from a heart attack, and Al and Jean Tirman were out of town, visiting their children. But everyone else came, and they all were wearing their club jackets. I also saw most of them in the social hall, mingling."

"Wasn't Darren Harwood the board president prior to Ralph Blackstone? I have to ask him about something. Has he fully recovered?"

"Yeah, he was board president before Ralph. And you can talk to him; he's doing fine and is back to all his normal activities. I'll give you Darren's cell phone number."

"Thanks. And Mel, please don't take offense, but I have to ask. Would you and Mike be able to say you had airtight alibis for the time of the murder, as you were at the YMC desk?"

"Of course I'm not offended. You've put your finger on the big problem with this murder. Both Mike and I would repeatedly leave the table to schmooze with new people or to get some sangria— I've discovered I drink a lot more sangria when it's free! Of course, it was pretty cheap stuff, but what would you expect? We would make sure one person was always at the YMC table. This behavior pattern was typical of virtually everyone manning the tables, as well as the other people there. Virtually no one has a verifiable alibi for the time of the murder, which was roughly the period between three ten and three thirty. And of course, most people weren't checking their watches too often to note the time. It wouldn't have taken more than three or four minutes for someone to briskly walk over to the club room, whack Max with the bat, and return to the social hall."

Amy nodded. "Makes sense. Did Max get along well with the other club members?"

Mel smiled. "No. He was a loud boor who always tried to show off his baseball knowledge, which he obviously could have just looked up on the Internet. He tried to get people to bet him about sports trivia. And he was a big Mets fan, which was fine, but he liked to bad-mouth the Yankees in a way that was very offensive. Two former YMC members told me that they had quit the club because of Max. But I think our current members had reached the point where they found him morbidly amusing or at least tolerable.

"On the plus side, Max was willing to go the extra mile for the club. He helped a lot with the clerical work—you know, sending out notices and other stuff like that. And, amazingly, he actually got Ed Kranepool to come and speak!"

"I guess I should be embarrassed to ask this," said Amy, "but who's Ed Kranepool?"

Mel laughed. "He's a guy from the Bronx who joined the Mets at the end of their first season, in 1962, when he was only seventeen years old. He played with the Mets for his whole seventeen-year career. But don't be embarrassed. I wouldn't expect someone your age to know about Ed Kranepool, even if you were a base-ball fan."

"Well, I'm not too big of a baseball fan, but I do know who Yogi Berra is!"

Mel laughed again. "Yeah, that would make sense. Yogi Berra became famous beyond the world of baseball. Anyhow, it is inconceivable that any member of the YMC would have murdered Max."

Amy smiled. "Well, someone killed him. Was Max a member of any other clubs?"

Mel nodded. "I know he was a member of the Men's Discussion Group. He had been a widower for several years, but he told me he was not a member of the Singles Club—he said he had once gone to one of their meetings and found all the women there disgusting. As for any other clubs, I can't tell you. He was an active shuffle-board player, but I don't think there's an actual club for that."

"Is your wife, Annette, a member of the YMC?"

"No, she's originally from Edmonton, Alberta, and she's never been a baseball fan. On the afternoon Max was killed, she was at a shopping mall with some girlfriends."

"Is there anything else you can tell me that might help me in my investigation?"

"Not that I can think of. If I think of something else, I'll definitely contact you. And again, I'm so very grateful to you for agreeing to help. Of course, I understand that nothing may come of it. But even if Max was not the most likeable guy, people should care about his being murdered and should want his killer brought to justice."

When Amy arrived back at her hotel at eleven thirty, she found her husband doing actuarial computations on his computer. She kissed him and he explained. "Sweetheart, I have a client that just emailed me with a significant problem that can't wait."

"Can you talk now?"

Jeremy nodded. "Sure, I meant it can't wait until we get back home. I have a few days to work things out for my client, but it will take a decent amount of time. Hopefully, I can still get in some tennis."

Amy proceeded to describe her conversation with Mel. "So, Jerry, what are your first impressions?"

"Well, to start, Mel obviously didn't kill Max; he's the one who asked you to get involved."

Amy nodded. "That's for sure."

"Also, we have only Ralph's word that he brought the box in and saw Max alive at around ten after three. We do have Mike, who was with Ralph at two forty-five and spoke to Max at the YMC desk, so we can be quite sure Max was alive then."

Amy nodded again. "You have a point. I should verify the two forty-five sighting of Max with Mike. But unless Ralph is the killer—which I seriously doubt—why should he lie? I'll stick with the murder being between ten past three and three thirty."

"Okay, in that case, I'm assuming someone saw Max walk into the empty club room at something like two forty-five, and that person waited at least twenty-five minutes to go in there and murder him. But the killer would know that the longer they waited, the more likely it would be that other YMC members would arrive at the club room. So why wait?"

"But Jerry, what if the killer was not in the YMC and didn't know about the four o'clock movie?"

"Yes, but if the killer saw Max enter the club room, peeked in, and saw him alone, why wait?"

"Well, there were no fingerprints on the bat. Maybe the killer peeked in and saw Max as well as the bat, so the killer went home to put on a pair of gloves before returning to use the bat on Max, so as to guarantee no prints."

Jeremy kissed his wife. "See, I was right in what I said at the presentation; you are the smart one in the marriage! However, I have another question, which also came up in the Lido Deck case. Based on what Mel told you, and also what Ralph said, you're probably gonna find tons of residents who strongly disliked Max. But—unless you discover otherwise—nobody tried to kill him for years, until this past January 31. What happened on that date to suddenly get the killer to act?"

Amy smiled. "I'm impressed that you see the connection with the Lido Deck case. Maybe someone's continued negative encounters with Max gradually built up, so that person's hatred for Max reached the critical mass to get them to act on murdering him on January 31. In the Lido Deck case, there were many years of no encounters with the victim. But still, your point is something to think about."

"So, sweetheart, who will you interview next?"

"Actually, I'm going to do something of a detour from the actual murder case. You remember that Ralph told me the rule is that the elected board president gets to select the activities chair? It just seems so weird to me. Ralph said he didn't know the reason for the rule. My parents also don't know. The board president prior to

Ralph was Darren Harwood. I want to ask him if he knows why that rule was instituted."

Jeremy had an idea. "Maybe the residents of the community didn't want the people holding those two positions to be at odds with each other. They wanted things to run as smoothly as possible."

Amy nodded. "Possibly. Let me make a phone call to Darren and request a meeting, hopefully this afternoon."

Saturday, March 21, 2015, p.m.

At five past three in the afternoon, Amy Bell and Darren Harwood sat in Darren's dining room, sipping wine. "Thank you, Amy, for accepting the murder case. You definitely didn't have to put yourself through this, and I am very grateful that you did. This murder is a stain on our community, and if the killer is not identified, the stain will be greater."

"Darren, I appreciate those words. First, I was told you suffered a heart attack in January. Are you okay now?"

"Yes, although things were touch-and-go for a few hours. It occurred on January 29. I was going from door to door, campaigning for board president. It was a week before the election. I guess I pushed myself too hard. Anyhow, I stayed in the hospital for five nights. My wife, Christine—she's currently out shopping with Annette Barton—visited me for two and a half hours every morning, bringing me her good cheer. And every afternoon at about two fifteen, she called me from the clubhouse café to tell me what was going on in the clubhouse, as well as the latest gossip. The doctor would generally call her from the hospital sometime between four and six to update her on my condition. She would call me again at seven to go over how I was doing. The doctors were fantastic. I don't want to dwell on the medical details. I'm fine now, but I've been ordered to slow my pace a bit."

Amy interrupted. "I have spoken to Ralph Blackstone, and he is the board president. So I guess you lost the election."

"That I did. I guess the people who voted for me out of sympathy were outnumbered by those who voted against me because they felt that I would no longer be able to put enough energy into the job. I think I might have won if it weren't for the heart attack."

"Darren, I understand you actually were, at one time, the board president. Is that correct?"

"Yes. We moved here from Chicago seven years ago. We have no children, and both of us had retired—at a pretty young age, in our fifties—from careers where we managed and interacted with lots of people, so an active adult community like this was perfect for us. In 2010, the previous board president declined to run for reelection. Christine convinced me to run, mainly because she wanted to be chairperson of the activities committee."

Amy laughed. "Actually, that's why I wanted to speak to you. This is way out on a tangent, but I heard about the rule that the board president selects the activities chair. That rule struck me as highly unusual. I asked Ralph why they had such a rule, and he told me he had no idea. So, do you know how the rule came about?"

Darren shook his head. "No, the rule was there when we arrived, which was three years after the builder turned the community over to the residents. And as the rule would help Christine get the position she wanted, we didn't ask anybody why it was in place."

"How long did you serve as board president?"

"Two years. Then Ralph beat me in the February 2012 election. He disagreed with me on certain community priorities, and he was an excellent, personable campaigner. I wish I had his natural ability to campaign. Anyhow, I still think he's wrong about the priorities, and in the 2013 and 2014 elections, I ran again, and Ralph beat me, but by diminishing margins. As I said, I could well have beaten him this year, except for the heart attack. But if it wasn't for Christine badly wanting to regain the activities chair, I probably would have retired gracefully after my 2012 defeat and not run again."

"Will you run again next year?"

"At this point, I can't say. But if I do run, there will have to be other people going from door to door campaigning for me, and doing the grunt work if I'm elected. I'm willing to be the brains, but no longer the brawn."

Amy laughed. "Do you have any suggestions as to who I can ask about the origin of the rule?"

Darren smiled. "As a matter of fact, I do. I'm phoning Dave Bosworth. He's been here since the beginning. Let me see if I can get him on the phone." Darren punched in the number.

"Hi Dave, it's Darren. I'm here with Amy Bell, and she has a question. Let me put her on the phone."

Amy got on and asked her question, and Dave laughed. "Amy, I do know the reason for the rule. During the first year that the residents ran the community, the board president and the activities chair hated each other. They were constantly at each other's throats and actually came to blows at one point. After the next February election, the new board president proposed the rule, and it was passed overwhelmingly in a communitywide vote to become part of the bylaws."

Amy thanked Dave for the information and hung up. She smiled at Darren. "That's basically what my husband had suggested. As I said in my presentation, he's a very smart guy. Now let me return to my actual investigation. I'd like you to tell me everything you can about Max."

"Well, I was in the hospital on the day he was killed, but as a general impression, I'd say he did everything possible to make sure people would dislike him. When I was board president, he would get up at public board meetings and complain about anything and everything. Other residents at the meetings would often shout him down, tell him to sit down and shut up, that kind of thing. I'm a member of the YMC—I'm a Cubs fan, but it was politically wise for me to join a large number of clubs—and Max was no fun there either. As a Mets fan, he always insulted the Yankees in crude ways, and he would belittle the baseball knowledge of other club members. I am not in the Men's Discussion Group, but if you want to hear some horror stories about Max's conduct there, I can tell you who to speak to. And there's a website called SDE Neighbors, where he posted messages insulting other posters, sometimes regarding politics, but more often regarding general community issues."

Amy laughed. "Sorry; this is not really funny, but I can't help myself. I think I get the picture. Is Christine also a member of the YMC?"

"No, the only sport she's interested in is volleyball. She plays volleyball here, in the regular Saturday morning ladies' game. And she's a damn good player; I've watched her play. Are you a baseball fan?"

"Not too much. My sport is—don't laugh—table tennis, and my husband's sport is tennis."

"You know, we have tennis courts here and also table tennis. You two can use them while you're here, as your father's guests."

After a few more minutes of amiable chitchat, Amy thanked Darren, departed, and drove back to the hotel, where Jeremy was still at work. She recounted what Darren had said. Jeremy made an observation. "You know, I'm certain there's people like Max in every active adult community."

Amy nodded. "Sounds like a standard type of jerk who craves attention, and the only way he knows how to get it is through antisocial behavior. If he somehow could have found a positive way to be listened to, I'll bet he would have embraced it."

Jeremy kissed his wife. "Yep, you've probably got Max pegged perfectly. But those kind of people generally don't get their heads bashed in with baseball bats."

"You're right, but it only takes one killer to buck that trend. I think we should speak to Dad before we all go out to the restaurant this evening. Let's see what he says about his good friend Max. Maybe he'll give us a different perspective."

At four forty-five, Amy and Jeremy were seated with Amy's parents in their living room.

Irving was expounding on the topic of Max Gattner. "Max and I both came from Queens. He moved here with his wife a year before we did. I originally met him playing shuffleboard, a few weeks after we arrived. His wife had died three months before. They had been, for some time, estranged from their only child, so Max was basically alone.

"Max had retired from a career in the men's clothing business. His wife had been a nurse. She had also inherited some money. Max cared about working people, and he understood how our society was rigged to further aggrandize the rich. He cared about minorities, and he understood how the system was set up to keep them down."

"In other words," interrupted Jeremy with a smile, "he agreed with you, politically."

"That's true. But there was a difference. I did not find it necessary to publicize my views among the residents of our community. This is because I can frequently discuss politics with my family, specifically with Carole, Jacob, and Simon. And, less frequently, with you, Amy. And of course, occasionally—in a different way—with Jeremy." Everyone laughed.

"But Max didn't have that kind of family support group. Sure, he had Carole and me, but that wasn't enough for him. He needed to spread his strong political views—as well as his various other opinions—around. And he did it aggressively, in the Men's Discussion Group and on the SDE Neighbors website.

"He also didn't have much sympathy in general for stupid people, or for stupid things going on in the community. But where I might agree with him, I would hold my tongue. Max would not. He called them all out. But Max was a good and decent person, someone who truly cared."

Carole chimed in. "I agree; Max was a good man. He had his faults, but he was a good man."

Amy and Jeremy smiled at each other.

"Dad, I know Max was a member of the YMC and also the Men's Discussion Group. Was he in any other clubs?"

"Yes, the Billiards Club. I'm also in that club, although I only show up for their club hours about half the time. Interestingly, when Max was in the billiard room, he avoided controversies. It was like a peaceful refuge for him. In addition to the club hours, he would show up at other times when he'd be all alone. He'd rack up the balls and practice."

"Dad, are you in the Men's Discussion Group, and do you or Mom post on the SDE Neighbors website?"

"I'm not in the Men's Discussion Group. I attended several meetings a few years ago, but for some reason, I wasn't comfortable there. We do read the postings on the SDE Neighbors website, but we rarely post."

"Max's wife had been dead for several years. Was he dating?"

"I asked Max that question a while ago. He said he preferred to keep that kind of information private. I never saw him with a woman in any situation that would imply they might be dating. So maybe he was just too embarrassed to tell me he wasn't dating anyone—not that he should have been embarrassed." Irving glanced at his watch. "Now, I think it's time to head for the restaurant."

The foursome arrived at Adamo's Restaurant at five thirty. They were escorted to a table for twelve in a private room in the back. Within ten minutes, they were joined by Amy's brothers, Simon and Jacob, and their wives and children, and the table was full.

The children, all teenagers, expressed perfunctory congratulations to Irving and Carole on the occasion of their forty-fifth anniversary, but they were mainly interested in Amy's detective work. This caused Amy no small amount of embarrassment; she wanted it to be her parents' evening. She satisfied them by recounting the details of what she called the Letter-Perfect case, and how she solved it and brought the killer to justice.

Amy noted that something Jeremy said had given her the key to solving the case. "He's so smart!" she exclaimed.

"Is that why you married Jeremy?" inquired Daniel, Jacob's sixteen-year-old son.

Amy smiled broadly. "No, I married Jerry because he is the sexiest man in the world!"

Everyone laughed.

Amy, Jacob, and Simon announced their joint anniversary gift to their parents, a luxury one-week Hawaii vacation, plus fancy Tissot his-and-hers watches.

For dessert, a chocolate cake was brought out, with "Happy forty-fifth anniversary, Carole and Irving!" written on it.

Sunday, March 22, 2015

At 1:00 p.m., Amy Bell was sitting across from Ralph Blackstone in the board office at the clubhouse. Amy decided that Ralph, despite being about five inches shorter than Bill Clinton, reminded her of the former president, because of his face and manner of speaking.

"Ralph, you mentioned that you had put on a Mets cap for the YMC film. Are you actually a Mets fan?"

"Oh yes; I was born in Astoria, Queens. I went to Bryant High School. Then I attended Fairleigh Dickenson University—that's where I met Susan—and we stayed in New Jersey after that, until we moved here. Susan is originally from New Jersey; sadly, she isn't interested in baseball."

"Wow!" exclaimed Amy. "I grew up in Newtown, Queens—technically it's Elmhurst—but I lived in Astoria for three and a half years, until I married Jerry and we moved to Greenwich Village. I was on Twenty-Ninth Street. Where were you?"

"We lived on Forty-Third Street. Small world!"

"Anyhow, I'd like you to walk me to the social hall, and then to club room B, and take me inside."

"Sure, let's do it."

Amy timed them as they walked from the social hall entrance to the door of the club room. At a moderate pace, the walk took forty-five seconds. They then entered the room.

"Can you show me the chair where you found Max's body?"

"Yes, it's this one. The furniture hasn't been moved since then." Amy observed a comfortable-looking, well-cushioned chair, facing toward the front of the room—where the film would have been shown—and facing away from the entrance door, which was in the rear of the room. Amy noted that where the murder weapon had previously been, on the rear table, there was now a baseball glove, in a locked glass case.

"The glove is signed by Phil Rizzuto," explained Ralph. "It was generously donated to the YMC, two weeks ago, by one of the members. There were some people in the club who felt—for reasons I cannot understand—that the club should get another bat, but they were outvoted."

"Was the Yogi Berra bat always kept on that table, and did the general SDE community know about the bat and where it was located?"

Ralph nodded. "When the bat was acquired, about a year ago, it was placed permanently on the club room table. The event was pretty well publicized. I can't say what percentage of the community would have recalled this information on this past January 31."

Amy noted two other doors, on one side of the club room, with a large M and W, respectively, on them.

"The club room has its own restrooms?"

"Yes and no. Both restrooms have two exit doors. One exit leads out to the hall, and one leads to this club room. So the restrooms are actually for all clubhouse visitors. There is one other club room with the same restroom setup. Why don't you go into the ladies' restroom and take a look? The men's restroom is the same, except that one stall is replaced by...well, you know."

Amy walked over and entered the ladies' restroom. There were three stalls and a sink. She opened the other exit door and found herself in the hall. For a few seconds, she couldn't figure out where she was in relation to the club room door through which she had originally entered. Then she realized that she'd have to go down the hall and turn left to get back to the original door, which is exactly what she did. Then she reentered the club room.

"Ralph, that's an ingeniously functional restroom arrangement!"

"You bet. Actually, as I recall, on January 31, after I put down the box with the baseball caps, here in the club room, I had to use the restroom, so I went into the men's room and exited from there into the hall."

Amy smiled. "Makes sense. I would like to take a look inside Max's house. Will that be possible?"

"Actually, as board president, I have two sets of Max's house and car keys, until such time as his heir takes possession. You can borrow a set—I'll get it for you when we get back to the office—and you can go into his house. But the authorities still have his cell phone, an old-style flip phone, and his computer. I've been told they've found nothing useful on them. By the way, Max didn't have a landline phone, and he never texted."

"Who is his heir?"

"Max was a widower with one child, a son. As far as I know, he left no will. So I assume his son will inherit."

Amy nodded. "Also, do you have the name of someone in law enforcement I can contact about Max's killing?"

"Yes, my contact is Deputy Sheriff Alan Richie. I'll tell him about you, and I'll give you his contact information. I'm sure he'll assist you in any way he can."

Back in the board office, Ralph gave Amy the keys, as well as the contact information for the deputy sheriff. "I'll phone him at nine fifteen tomorrow morning. And you should know that everyone on the board of directors thanks you for your efforts. We are realistic about your likelihood of any success, but we are praying for a miracle."

Amy returned to the hotel before her husband, who was playing tennis. When he arrived back, at three o'clock, he was tired but happy. "Those guys may be old, but they're good! I got beat, but I think I gave a good account of myself."

She related her discussion with Ralph. "So I can check out Max's house anytime I want. I think I'll try to meet with the deputy sheriff as soon as possible. Ralph said the authorities found nothing useful on Max's computer and phone—they still have them in their possession—but I want to know what 'non-useful' things they found."

"Sweetheart, you say it took only forty-five seconds to walk from the social hall to the club room?"

"Yes. And tons of people in the community knew the bat was there. So it would be feasible for so many people to leave the social hall, kill Max with the bat, and get back to the social hall only a couple of minutes later, without having been missed."

"Provided they knew Max was in the club room. And apparently, virtually no one knew."

Amy nodded. "Unless the killer happened to be in the hall at the time and saw Max go into the club room. I'm assuming that's what happened; it seems to be the only reasonable explanation. But then, as we had discussed, the killer waited at least twenty-five minutes to go in there and kill Max. Despite the explanation that the killer might have gone home to get gloves, I'm not comfortable about that time gap. I keep thinking that I'm missing something critically important."

"Well, sweetheart, it's early in the investigation; we've only just begun."

Amy gave her husband a playful smooch on the cheek. "A kiss for luck, and we're on our way!"

"What made you say that?"

Amy stroked Jeremy's cheek. "Poor, poor boy; you should know! Think about it for a while, and tell me when you've figured it out."

The big anniversary celebration was held in the banquet hall of the Desert Oasis Hotel. There were about one hundred guests. First, there was a lavish dinner. Just before dessert, there were several congratulatory speeches, and then Irving and Carole spoke. Following the meal, there were two hours of music from a band and lots of dancing and drinking.

As the event was nearing its conclusion, Amy's brothers, Jacob and Simon, asked Jeremy if they could talk to him privately. The three men exited the banquet hall and stood in the hotel lobby. Jacob looked very solemn as he spoke. "Jeremy, we got hold of a recording which was made secretly. I'd rather not say how we got it or who recorded it. We need your advice, as to what to do."

Jeremy was nonplussed. "What's on the recording? Can I hear it?"

"Well, we don't have it with us, but Simon can tell you exactly what it says."

Jeremy turned toward Simon.

"Okay, here goes. I'm giving you advance notice. This will be painful and upsetting for you to hear. It's a recording, from 1988, of President Reagan saying, 'Screw the poor! I've been shafting them for eight years, and they are too dumb to realize it. We've succeeded brilliantly in helping the rich get richer!' Jeremy, should we give the recording to the media?"

Before Jeremy could think of a response, the brothers burst out laughing. "Gotcha!" they said simultaneously, and they ran back toward the banquet hall. Jeremy decided it was best to just let them have their fun. He shook his head and smiled as he slowly headed back.

When it was all over, they returned to the Mesa Suites Hotel. Jeremy gave his wife a big hug. "Sweetheart, that was great! Your parents should be very happy."

"For sure! Now the only thing remaining for us here is the minor matter of Max's murder." Amy laughed.

Her husband grinned broadly. "Yes, but no worries. We'll start out walking and learn to run."

Amy smiled as she stroked Jeremy's cheek. "Good boy; you've figured out what I was saying earlier!"

"Yep, the Carpenters song. At the presentation, you announced that I was smart. So I had to live up to that."

"Well, at yesterday's dinner, I also announced that you are the sexiest man in the world. Because of that attribute, and because you figured out the significance of my previous comment, I am now incredibly hot for you! So you had better get into action, immediately, to address my condition."

Jeremy immediately got into action.

Monday, March 23, 2015, a.m.

At ten forty in the morning, Amy Bell sat down across from Alan Richie at the local office of the county sheriff. She and the deputy sheriff shook hands and agreed to use first names.

"Thank you, Alan, for seeing me on such short notice."

"No problem. Ralph Blackstone tells me you're one of the top private detectives in New York City. How long will you be here in Arizona?"

"Ralph is very kind. I'll be here for no more than nine more days. I've got to be back home and at work by April second. My husband and I came here to celebrate my parents' forty-fifth wedding anniversary. Then, when we arrived, some people in their community recruited me to look into the murder of Max Gattner."

"Well, even for someone with your truly superior investigative talents"—Amy decided, from Alan's tone of voice and facial expressions, that he didn't really believe any of that—"it doesn't give you too much time."

"That's an understatement. I accepted the case with everyone understanding that the most likely result will be that I won't find out anything new. And I have emphasized that fact when I've spoken to Ralph, as well as some other residents. Anyhow, I will be very grateful for all the details you can provide regarding Max's murder."

"Sure." Alan referred to his notes. "On January 31, at 3:33 p.m., our office received a phone call about the body being found in the club room. Our people arrived at 3:49. The dead man—later determined to be age sixty-six, five feet, nine inches tall, and one hundred fifty-four pounds—was identified by many persons in the room, and by identification in his wallet, as Max Gattner. It was also later determined to be overwhelmingly likely that he died in the period between two forty and three thirty. Of course, based on the information provided by Ralph Blackstone, the time of the murder was clearly between three ten and three thirty.

"He had apparently been struck from behind on the top of the head. He had probably been struck three times. The murder weapon was later verified to be the baseball bat that was lying near the body. There were no fingerprints on the bat. The only blood and DNA found on the bat was that of the victim. The police found a Bic Soft Feel retractable ballpoint pen, with black ink, under the table where the bat had been. Maybe the killer somehow dropped it while grabbing the bat, and it rolled under the table. Or maybe it belonged to someone else. But there was no useful material found on the pen.

"I did call and ask the president of the Yankees/Mets Club to casually mention, at their next meeting, that someone told him they had found a pen in the club room, and to ask if anyone at the meeting had lost a pen. I said not to mention that the sheriff had the pen. He called back several days later and told me he had done as I had requested, and no one said they had lost a pen."

Amy changed the subject. "Was there any evidence of a struggle or that Max realized he was about to be struck by the bat?"

"None whatsoever. The killer may have entered quietly and come up behind Max without him realizing it. Or maybe Max was taking a nap. His blood had a significant alcohol level—people said they saw him drinking awhile earlier, in the social hall—so that may have made him a bit tired."

"Could they determine whether the killer was a lefty or a righty?"

"No. The best guess is that the killer gripped the bat with both hands and swung the bat in a straight downward direction onto Max's head."

"I understand that you still have Max's phone and computer. Can you tell me what you found there?"

"I'll give you the printout of all his incoming and outgoing phone numbers for the months of December and January. The printout also identifies the other parties. We didn't find anything unusual there. With regard to his computer, the main item of interest was his activity on the SDE Neighbors website."

"Alan," Amy interjected, "can you print out for me all the messages on that website which he sent or which were responses or were otherwise related to him?"

"Yes, I'll get you those messages for this past December and January. Max—as well of some of the other posters—used some very nasty language. We did speak to the people he was exchanging insults with, but nothing useful came of that."

"What about Max's actual emails?"

"Absolutely nothing of interest."

"Was Max involved with Facebook or Twitter or the like?"

"No. The only social-media site he was involved with, aside from SDE Neighbors, was Modern Progressive America. It's a very liberal website, and Max posted frequently—sometimes ten posts in one day. But he didn't get into any disputes on that site; everyone who posted was on the same side of the political spectrum. Would you like the printout from that site? I can also send you his emails."

Amy nodded. "Yes, I'd like those; thank you. I presume you also spoke to the people who were in the clubhouse around the time of the murder."

"Of course. But they were running a club event in the social hall at the time, and people were constantly walking around, mingling. Almost nobody who was there had an ironclad alibi for the time of the murder. From what we were told, almost everyone in the community who knew Max disliked him. So there are countless suspects and very little evidence."

"Alan, let me tell you what's been bothering me, and please tell me if you have any ideas. At two forty-five, Max told Mel Barton and Mike Whelan—at the YMC desk in the social hall—that he was feeling a bit dizzy and was proceeding at that time to the club room."

"Yes, we confirmed this with Mel and Mike. They saw him leaving the social hall just after they spoke to him."

"Is it correct that no one saw Max alive after that time, except, of course, for Ralph Blackstone—who brought in the box of caps between five and ten after three—and the killer?"

"Yes, that's correct, as far as we know. We interviewed over a hundred people, and none reported having seen Max after two forty-five, except for Ralph."

"So," Amy continued, "it looks like the killer happened to be in the hall at around two forty-five and saw Max enter the club room.

Then the killer waited at least twenty-five minutes to enter the club room and kill Max. That doesn't make sense to me. I realize the killer might have gone home to get gloves, so as to avoid fingerprints, but that somehow doesn't ring true. What do you think?"

Alan thought for a few seconds. "I'm impressed that a bigshot detective like you is interested in the opinion of a deputy sheriff."

Amy was annoyed by this attitude, but she knew how to respond. "On the contrary, the police authorities I've worked with in New York have been some of the smartest and most perceptive people I have ever known, and I am very anxious to hear any opinions you may have."

The deputy sheriff appeared to be assuaged. "Well, the obvious possibility is that Max entered the room at around two forty-five, but then he exited for some reason at a later time and was observed by the killer when he reentered the room. This exit and reentry by Max would have been after Ralph had put down the box with the caps and left the club room."

Amy nodded. "That is, indeed, a possibility."

Alan continued. "Also, the killer might have had other obligations during the period immediately following observing Max entering the club room. For example, maybe the killer was with some people in the hall at two forty-five, and the killer—but probably not the others—noticed Max entering the club room at that time. But the killer was stuck with those people for the next thirty minutes or so."

Amy smiled. "Yes, that is also a possibility."

"Or maybe the killer didn't realize—at the time they saw Max go in—that Max would be the only person in the club room. Then, after a period of time, it dawned on the killer that Max might be alone, and in that case, there would be a good opportunity to kill him."

Amy thought for a few seconds. "Yeah, that could be."

Alan rose. "If there's any other way I can help you, please don't hesitate to contact me. I'll have all the printouts delivered to your hotel by the end of the day."

"That's perfect. Thank you so much for all your assistance." Amy provided her hotel information, shook hands with the deputy sheriff and departed.

At eleven forty-five, she found her husband in their hotel room, working on the computer. "So, sweetheart, how did your meeting go with the deputy sheriff?"

Amy went through the details of her conversation with Alan. Then she made a phone call. "Hi Ralph, it's Amy Bell. I have a question. When you brought the box with the hats into the club room, did Max appear to be alert, or did he appear to be somewhat tired?"

"He definitely appeared tired, probably from drinking too much sangria in the social hall. I had the impression he was just about ready to take a little nap."

"One more question. Does the clubhouse order a specific brand of pen, to be used for the various staff and activities there?"

"Yes, the pens we use are Bic Soft Feel retractable, with black ink. Residents 'borrow' them from reception and the café, and wherever else we leave them around, so we keep having to order more."

"Thanks, Ralph." Amy got off the phone. "So at least one of Alan's possible explanations for the time gap is probably no good. Max probably didn't leave the room after Ralph left. He was tired and probably took a nap, so he never heard the killer enter and come up behind him."

Jeremy nodded. "Sounds likely. What about Alan's other possible explanations?"

"Well, it's possible that the killer was talking to other people when Max went in, or the killer didn't realize until thirty minutes later that Max might be alone. But that implies the killer was intent on killing Max on that day, if possible. Otherwise, the killer wouldn't have bothered going back to the club room at a later time to do the deed."

"So, you're rejecting all three of Alan's explanations?"

"I'm not saying they're impossible, just quite unlikely. The same with the idea that the killer went home to get gloves."

"But there has to be some sort of explanation, given the fact that Max *was* murdered. So maybe one of those four explanations is correct, despite having been unlikely. After all, long shots do sometimes win horse races."

"Okay, Jerry, you have a point."

"Sweetheart, what about the Bic pen?

"Ralph said that's the pen they use in the clubhouse, so it's not apt to help me. It's a very popular pen. I think I myself have a few in my desk in our apartment. Now, why don't you accompany me to visit Max's house?"

Jeremy gave her an extended hug. "You've got a deal."

Monday, March 23, 2015, p.m.

Max Gattner's house, on Panorama Lane, was the same model as that of Amy's parents. At two fifteen, Amy unlocked the front door, and she and Jeremy began nosing around.

Amy found nothing of interest in the living and dining rooms. She observed the photos of Max with his late wife in the den. In that room, there were also two presidential campaign posters on the wall—one for George McGovern and another for Barack Obama. *Wow,* thought Amy, *this guy had political views very similar to mine!*

Then she checked out the master bedroom and the master bath, which was *en suite*. The master bath had two sinks, what Irving had described as "his and hers." It was clear which sink Max was using. His shaver and shaving accessories were on the sink's counter, as well as deodorant and men's aftershave lotion. There was a tube of toothpaste and an electric toothbrush. There was also a soap dispenser.

The other sink counter had very few items on it. There was a standard toothbrush as well as a soap dish, upon which was placed a well-used bar of soap. Amy sniffed the soap and was surprised by the perfumed fragrance. She opened the door to the storage cabinet below the sink. The only things she found inside were a spray bottle of all-purpose cleaner and an unopened bar of J'adore Silky Soap by Dior. Amy took out the bar, unwrapped it, and sniffed the fragrance. Then she again sniffed the used bar. It was the same scent. She took the bars with her and showed the unused bar to her husband when she met back up with him in the kitchen.

"Jerry, I want you to sniff this soap bar, which I found in the master bath, and then tell me what you think."

Jeremy followed instructions and then said, "Ladies' soap."

"You bet! It's J'adore soap by Dior. It's a high-priced, ultra-luxurious, perfumed ladies' soap. There was also this used bar on a soap dish on one of the bathroom sinks. Max's wife died several years ago. Why are these two soap bars in the master bath? Don't say they were for use by his wife, because the used soap is not all dried out and crumbled, the way it would be after years of disuse.

"By the way, in the master bedroom walk-in closet, there are two bathrobes, and one of them has a floral design on it, so it is a woman's robe. There are also two pairs of slippers, and one pair looks like it would be for a woman. Of course, the robe and slippers could theoretically have been his wife's, but not the used soap. So, tell me more about what you think."

"Clearly, Max had a lady friend who frequently slept over. Or possibly she frequently came over for visits of multiple hours' duration during the day."

Amy smiled. "I'm going for the lady sleeping over, although your second idea can't be completely rejected out of hand. However, my father said he never saw Max with that kind of lady friend. So that means Max and the lady didn't want anyone to find out, so they never appeared in the community together."

"Sweetheart, are you suggesting that the lady is married, possibly to someone in this community?"

"Yes, Jerry, that's exactly what I'm suggesting, and I think it's quite likely that his lady friend and her husband live in this community."

Jeremy nodded. "In that case, I think you'll be very interested in what I found in the garage." He led his wife into the laundry room, and from there through the door directly into the garage. The only vehicle there was a 2013 Honda Accord, which had been modified to have a privacy divider between the front and back seats. The windows for the back seat also had privacy glass, as did the rear windshield.

Amy smiled. "So Max made sure that no one could see his lady passenger, who sat in the back, and they drove into his garage and entered his house from the garage into the laundry room."

"Can we somehow find out the identity of that lady? Her husband would be one hell of a suspect, as would be the lady herself."

"Well, I'll be receiving Max's phone and email records later today. I'll start with them. But I want to see what my father knows about the Honda." She punched in the number on her cell phone and put on the speakerphone.

"Hi, Dad. I have you on speakerphone for Jerry to hear. Have you come back to earth yet after yesterday's big affair?"

"Not fully. But your mother and I are already planning for our Hawaii vacation. And you and your brothers shouldn't have gone overboard by spending all that money on our anniversary gifts."

Amy smiled. She had actually volunteered to put up half the money, with her brothers putting up one quarter each, but her dad didn't need to know that.

"It was our great pleasure; just enjoy! Jerry and I are at Max's house, looking for clues. What do you know about his uniquely modified Honda Accord?"

"Yeah, I know the whole story. He bought the car in October 2013. He knew the 2014s were coming soon, and he thought he could get a good price on a new 2013 Accord. The Honda dealer told Max that this particular car had been modified for a special order, but somehow the deal had fallen through. Max said the dealer offered him a nice extra discount if he would buy the car as is, and he accepted. Max never could resist a great deal, moneywise. When he bought the Accord, he sold his 2010 Civic."

"Okay, Dad, you can go back to planning for Hawaii."

Amy got off the phone. "So, Max must have started secretly seeing this woman shortly before he bought the Accord. And of course, there was no deal that fell through; Max must have made a special order for the dealer to put in the modifications."

Jeremy was confused. "Why didn't Max just bring the Civic in for the required modifications? I don't see the reason for him to buy a new car."

"He didn't modify his old car because some people in the community would realize what he had done, and that would arouse suspicion. But Max getting a great deal on a new car wouldn't raise any eyebrows."

Jeremy nodded. "That makes sense. This means Max had probably been having this married woman sleep over at his house for well over a year. Obviously, her husband must be away from home a lot."

"Yes, he probably has a job that frequently requires staying overnight in other cities. At the very least, he is out of the house for many hours at a time. This should narrow down the field of possible lady friends who live in South Desert Estates. We're looking for a married lady whose husband is frequently away and who uses J'adore soap."

"How are you gonna find out if a lady uses J'adore soap?"

Amy smiled. "When I visit her at her home, I'll ask if I can use the bathroom."

Jeremy laughed. "Now why didn't I think of that?"

Amy stroked her husband's cheek. "Poor, poor boy! When I said at the presentation that you were smart, I should have clarified it; you're super smart in some areas, and super clueless in others, such as figuring out what brand of soap a lady prefers." They both burst out laughing.

Then Jeremy had another question. "We know how Max could get the lady into his house unobserved, and how when he drove her there, people would not see her in the back seat. But wouldn't there occasionally be witnesses when he drove his car to her house to pick her up, or if he met her at the clubhouse area or at some other location in the community?"

Amy nodded. "I had thought of that, but there would be ways to assure privacy in that regard. For example, there's a Walmart that's just five minutes from the SDE gatehouse. The lady could take an overnight bag and drive her car to that Walmart. Max could also drive there, and they could park right next to each other in the parking lot. Then the lady could get out of her car and into Max's car. The next day, Max could drive her back to the Walmart lot, and she could drive her car home. As her car is normally parked in her garage, nobody would know it wasn't there overnight."

"Makes sense. Why are you so confident that Max's lady friend lives in South Desert Estates?"

"Jerry, do you mean to suggest Max could have gone to the super-market, where he met and hit it off with a married lady who lives somewhere outside of SDE?"

"Yes, that's what I mean. Or maybe he met the lady in some way on the Modern Progressive America website."

Amy shook her head. "It's theoretically possible, but I don't buy it. I'm pretty sure he met the lady here—probably in the YMC, or the Billiards Club, or while playing shuffleboard. Or maybe he just happened to be sitting next to her at a clubhouse event.

"Anyhow, I'm looking forward to going through the phone num-bers and emails that the deputy sheriff is sending me; he said they'll be delivered to the hotel by the end of the day today. Hopefully, these will provide me with the identity of the lady. After all, they had to arrange the dates and times for their trysts."

"Did you tell me you'll also be receiving the postings from SDE Neighbors website, and also the progressive website?"

"Yes, but I'll put them aside for now. I want that lady's name; it's now my top priority."

The package from the county sheriff's office arrived at the hotel at six thirty in the evening. The reception desk called up to Amy's room and interrupted the couple as they were munching on a take-home pizza dinner from Romero's New York Style Pizza—which they both agreed was significantly less tasty than the pizza they ate back home.

When Amy opened the package, she was surprised at the small number of phone calls and emails Max had sent or received in the two-month period. On the other hand, she was shocked at the massive number of postings on the SDE Neighbors and on the Modern Progressive America websites. She made a decision.

"Jerry, I'm not going to go through all the postings on the progressive website. It's all people with the same politics. I simply don't have the time, and it is overwhelmingly likely that I'll get nothing useful out of any of it."

"Sweetheart, what about the SDE Neighbors?"

"We'll have to go through those, to get the names of the residents who were the targets of Max's nasty epithets or who used those epithets on him." Jeremy was not happy that Amy had used the word "we."

"However," Amy continued, "I'll put SDE Neighbors aside, until I identify Max's lady friend. She could be the key to solving the murder."

It took Amy less than half an hour to become terribly disappointed. The police had identified all the other parties for the phone calls. None of them were of any value. Nor were the emails.

Amy was intrigued by a total of thirty-one phone calls to Max from a phone number identified as belonging to the SDE clubhouse. She phoned Ralph to get an explanation, and she put him on speakerphone.

"Amy, there is a phone just to the right of the reception desk—you can check it out the next time you go there. It's available to be used by any resident to make a local call. The sign next to the phone says usage is limited to two calls per day, with each call limited to no more than two minutes. The people manning the reception desk sometimes have to gently remind residents of these rules, and that if there is too much abuse, the phone may have to be removed. But luckily, our residents have generally been cooperative. After all, most people have cell phones with unlimited calling for a flat fee."

Amy hung up and smiled at her husband. "So we now know how they made arrangements regarding dates, times, and pick-up points for their trysts. The lady phoned Max from the clubhouse. But these phone calls and emails I got from Alan are worthless."

Jeremy nodded. "Agreed on all counts. So, what's your next step?"

"Well, I want that lady! I'll start by contacting Mel. But I don't want to impose on him this evening; it may be a lengthy conversation. Let's just snuggle up together and watch TV. This has been a very busy day."

Tuesday, March 24, 2015, a.m.

At 10:00 a.m., Mel Barton answered his phone.

"Mel, this is Amy Bell."

"Hi, Amy. How's the investigation going?"

"Nothing to report yet. You're on speakerphone, so Jerry can hear. I need some information regarding the membership of the YMC. How many of the twenty-eight members are women?"

"There are five women."

"I need their names, approximate ages, and contact information. Also, I need anything you can tell me about their spouses or significant others. In particular, I need to know if the member's spouse is retired or employed."

"Wow, Amy, that's very mysterious. Can you tell me why you want this info?"

"Mel, I hope you'll understand that I can't explain anything at this time."

"Okay, I have all the records here in my den, so I can give you their phone numbers and emails. First there's Jean Tirman. She's married to Al Tirman. They are both in their early seventies and are both retired. Al is also a member of the YMC. I think I previously mentioned to you that they were out of town on the day of the murder.

"Then there's Marian Lento and Audrey Zackov. They are widows, in their seventies, and I know they hang out a lot with each other. They are both from New York, and they are both rabid Yankee fans. I would seriously doubt that either of them has a significant other.

"Wendy Frost is in her late fifties. Her husband, Arthur Frost, is also a YMC member. He works in Phoenix as a stockbroker. And Arlene McKay is in her sixties. Her husband, Ralph McKay, is not a YMC member. They are both retired. When I play tennis, I frequently see them playing tennis together."

Mel proceeded to give Amy the contact information for the five women.

"Mel, may I ask how well Max got along with Wendy when they were at the YMC meetings?"

"They didn't like each other. She's a big Yankees fan—she's originally from the Bronx—and Max would badmouth the Yankees and do it in ways that offended Wendy. Her husband Arthur would be amused by Max's antics, but Wendy often responded to Max by insulting the Mets, just to get Max as upset as she already was."

Amy had another question. "Mel, were there any ladies who may not have been YMC members, but who came to some of the YMC meetings?"

"Yes, as a matter of fact, there was one lady who came, for the first time, to our regular monthly meeting, at seven in the evening on Monday, January 26—the film on January 31 was a special event, in addition to the monthly meeting. She gave me her name and phone number; she said she might want to join. I didn't see her there for the film—of course, what with the murder, it was very hectic, and I might have missed her.

"Her name is Sharon Packney. She said she was divorced and had just moved to SDE in December from Seattle. She said she was a Mets fan, and she seemed very interested in Max. They were speaking to each other, and they left the meeting together. Besides Sharon, there were no other nonmember women who ever came to our meetings, as far as I can recall."

"What about the members who quit in the past few years? Were any of them women?"

"No, they were all men."

Mel gave Amy Sharon's number, and they got off the phone. Amy turned to her husband. "Well, Jerry, what do you think?

"Sweetheart, Wendy's husband works full time in Phoenix. She can't sleep over with Max, but she can be there for hours during the day, using the soap as well as the robe and slippers. She and Max could pretend to hate each other, so that her husband would never even imagine the possibility of his wife cheating on him with Max."

Amy nodded. "I originally thought the evidence favored a sleepover, but your scenario could be right on target. Then there's Sharon. She's obviously not Max's lady, as she just moved here from Seattle. But what if Max's lady saw Max and Sharon acting friendly together and got angry?"

Jeremy was confused. "If Max's lady is married and is cheating on her husband with Max, how can she be angry at Max seeing another woman?"

Amy smiled and stroked her husband's cheek. "Poor, poor boy! You have to understand that some women are not quite rational in situations like that. Anyhow, I think I'm going to call Sharon and try to meet with her."

Tuesday, March 24, 2015, p.m.

Sharon Packney's house on Belle View Drive was different from that of Amy's parents; the breakfast nook faced the front, rather than the back, and the entrance door was at the side of the house. Amy rang the bell at one fifteen and was welcomed by a shapely, attractive woman in her midfifties who was wearing several pieces of expensive jewelry. She was five feet, five inches tall and had medium-length black hair. She managed to smile while maintaining a businesslike expression.

Sharon escorted Amy to the living room. They sat in lavishly cushioned chairs, and Amy accepted a Diet Coke.

Sharon opened the conversation. "Amy, I saw your presentation. You were incredibly impressive. I am so grateful that you are investigating Max's killing. No one wants you to identify the murderer more than I do. That killer probably deprived me of a lot of fun."

Amy was intrigued. "Can you elaborate?"

Sharon smiled. "It is obvious, from your presentation—I also checked you out on the Web after you phoned me this morning— that you are a very intelligent and perceptive woman who understands the way the world works. So I don't have to mince words. I'm going to tell it to you like it is.

"I was married for twenty-five years to a man who was really big in Seattle real estate. But he wasn't big where it really mattered, if you know what I mean."

Amy laughed. "I'm pretty sure I know what you mean."

"Yes, Amy, I mean exactly what you think I mean. You spoke very highly of your husband, and of course, I saw him when he spoke. I'll bet he's big where it matters, right?"

Amy laughed again. "All I'll say is that Jerry and I are very happily married."

"Well, I'm a little envious. The last fifteen years of my marriage were mainly downhill. Then I caught him cheating—of course, I had been cheating on him for many years, but he never found out. Washington is a community-property state, so when we divorced, two years ago, I ended up a wealthy woman.

"I needed a dry climate for my health, and I have no problem with the heat, so I moved here. As an added bonus, I have a long-time gentleman friend who now lives in Phoenix. He's married, but he told me he'll be able to get away from her and see me at least twice a month.

"I decided to go to the meetings of a variety of clubs, to check out the available men. So I went to the YMC meeting on the evening of January 26. That's where I met Max. We talked, and we hit it off. We arranged to meet for lunch at the clubhouse café the next day at one o'clock. After lunch, we played shuffleboard. Then we came over to my house. Max was big where it mattered. I think we were both very pleased.

"I told Max I wanted us to be friends with benefits. No needy phone calls or texts or emails. No demands, no obligations, no strings. Max was completely happy with that arrangement. We agreed to meet again on the coming Sunday for lunch at the clubhouse café. It was understood what would happen after that. And then on that Saturday, the day before we were going to meet, Max was murdered."

"Sharon," Amy interrupted, "am I correct that lots of people saw you with Max on that Tuesday, the day after the YMC meeting?"

"Oh, yes. We were enjoying each other's company and didn't hide it. We waved hello to lots of people."

"Have you hit it off with any other men in the community?"

"Actually, not yet. I am making it a policy not to get involved in any way with SDE residents who are either married or have a significant other. As I want to get along with everyone here in the community, I think that's prudent."

Amy nodded. "Yes, that is indeed prudent."

"So my supply of eligible men here is limited. I've checked out many clubs, but I've discovered that my best opportunity to meet men is in the gym, where I exercise on the treadmill nearly every day. And I look very good when I'm exercising in the gym."

I'll bet you do! Amy thought. "Actually, Sharon, you look pretty damn good right now."

Sharon was beaming. "Thank you for saying that. You know, Amy, if you lived here, I'm sure we'd become great friends. I know you're currently busy with your investigation, but the next time you come here to visit your parents, let's be sure to get together. Maybe by then, I'll be nearly finished decorating the house. I think you'll be very impressed."

Amy nodded. "Sure, sounds good. So you haven't met any single guys in the gym?"

"So far, no luck. I've talked to a few single men there, but they just didn't click for me. However, I'm remaining optimistic. Anyhow, Max and I had clicked so well. His murder ruined everything for me."

And for Max, Amy thought. "Sharon, were you in the social hall, at the club event, on the day Max was murdered?"

"Yes, I was at the social hall, making the rounds of all the club desks. I left at around three thirty and went home. I found out about Max that evening."

Amy thanked Sharon for sharing her experiences and departed. Her next stop was at the home of Wendy Frost. Amy laughed to herself with the realization that her main goal would be to visit Wendy's master bath, checking for the brand of soap.

At two fifty, Wendy opened her front door, and Amy joined her hostess at the dining room table. Wendy was a petite woman with a round face and a big smile. She offered wine, and Amy accepted.

"Wendy, may I first make a weird request? My husband and I are renovating the master bath in our Manhattan apartment. I'm asking people here whose houses I visit if I can check out the sinks in their master bath to observe the counter colors and the faucet styles. Can I look at yours?"

Wendy laughed. "You're right, it's a bit weird, but it makes sense. No problem; follow me."

Upon entering the bathroom, it took about twenty seconds for Amy to ascertain that the soap bars on both sinks were not J'adore.

But she put on a big show of commenting on the beautiful counters and sleek faucets. Then the ladies returned to the dining room and to their red wine.

"Wendy, as I mentioned on the phone, I have been asked by Mel Barton and several other residents of the community to investigate the killing of Max Gattner. As he was murdered in club room B, just prior to the YMC's planned showing of a film, I felt I had to interview the members of the YMC."

Wendy nodded. "I saw your presentation, and I greatly admire you. I also admire your husband—in a different way." Both ladies burst out laughing. "But I am of two minds regarding your investigation. On the one hand, Max's murder was a terrible crime, and the killer should be caught and punished to the full extent of the law. On the other hand—and I hate myself for saying this—Max was a mean, nasty person, and this community is much better off without him. Surely you've spoken to other people here who have given you the same opinion of Max."

Amy nodded. "Yes, I have. But you don't believe, do you, that Max's boorishness at YMC meetings would cause some club member to decide to murder him?"

"No, I'm pretty sure that none of us in the YMC would have killed him. But his boorishness—as you've described it—extended to board meetings. I'm talking about the public ones, where all residents can attend. He was frequently a major disruptor there. Then, I know some guys in the Men's Discussion Group. They frequently had political discussions where Max hurled the ugliest epithets at people with conservative—or even moderate—views. Also, you should check out Max's postings on the SDE Neighbors website. His name-calling extended to anyone who disagreed with him about anything—not just politics."

Amy nodded again. "I appreciate what you're saying. Does your husband share your opinion of Max?"

"Arthur is a very mild-mannered guy. He's almost always calm, which is a big positive attribute when dealing with clients who are often nervous and tense and sometimes verbally abusive due to the ups and downs of the stock market. He usually just smiled when Max misbehaved at the YMC. But when we got back home, after we saw Max dead in the club room, he told me that while he was horrified by what he had seen, he was not unhappy that Max was dead."

Amy was contemplative. "Don't hate yourself for feeling the way you do. It's completely understandable. But I suspect that you—and most of the other SDE residents—would feel more comfortable if Max's murder case was solved, rather than if it remained unsolved."

Wendy was silent for a few seconds. Then she nodded and smiled. "When you put it that way, I think you're right." Wendy got up, and so did Amy; they shook hands. "I can see why you're a great detective. You have a way with people. We want to talk to you; we feel good talking to you."

Before returning to the hotel, Amy went to Walmart and purchased a rotisserie chicken and some salad and fruit, as well as a small chocolate cake. She got back to their room before Jeremy, who was playing tennis. He showed up at five fifteen, kissed his wife, and showered. Then they sat down at the table in their small kitchen, a feature of every accommodation at the Mesa Suites Hotel, and enjoyed chicken dinner. As they were finishing the chocolate cake, Amy updated her husband on her interviews with the two women. "So, Wendy was not Max's lady friend. And the other four female YMC members don't appear to be contenders for the role.

"By the way, I wanted to check the soap in the master bath, and I realized that if I just asked Wendy if I could use her bathroom, she would probably direct me to the guest bathroom. So I had to be more creative. I told her we were renovating our master bath, and I wanted to see her faucets and counters."

Jeremy smiled. "Well, based on your interview with Sharon, who-ever Max's lady friend was, she could easily have found out about him and Sharon. And by the way, Sharon sounds like one hell of a piece of work!"

Amy laughed. "That interview I had with Sharon is one of my all-time favorites. To say that she held nothing back is an under-statement! She even wanted me to comment on how big you are."

"Sweetheart, do you mean—"

"Yes, I mean exactly that. And don't worry, I didn't satisfy her curiosity."

"Well, now you've got me wondering about…you know."

Amy stroked her husband's cheek. "Poor, poor boy. I don't compare you to other men in that regard. Frankly, I don't even remember that kind of information, regarding any other men. After all, we got engaged to be married well over five years ago, and it's been only you since then. But I think it's time I did some more careful observation regarding this question."

Amy rose and quickly removed her shoes, blouse, and pants. She was now down to bra and panties, revealing her sexy, filled-out figure. She placed her hands on her hips. "Jerry, get all your clothes off, now! I'm going to do a thorough inspection and measurement."

Her husband realized he had little choice but to comply. Then Amy did some manual probing and announced her conclusion. "Jerry, I can confidently say that your measurement is substantially larger than it was a minute ago! Now I want you to retain that increased measurement for a period of time, while you satisfy all my desires. Then, when I'm completely satisfied, I will help you to reduce your measurement."

An hour later, Amy was completely satisfied, and Jeremy was completely exhausted. His measurement now reduced, they resumed their discussion regarding Amy's interviews.

Jeremy had an observation. "Based on what Sharon told you, and throwing in the mystery lady friend, Max was quite the stud, something one might not have expected based on the other things we know about him."

"So, you don't think loudmouth, bullying, progressive liberals can be attractive to the opposite sex?"

Jeremy didn't fall for this trap. "No, I was only referring to men with those characteristics. With regard to women, if they are attractive enough, a lot of men don't care about the other stuff. But even if this carries over to attractive men, Max was sixty-six years old. And we have his photo, which Ralph provided. I'm sure you'll agree he didn't look like a movie star."

Amy smiled. "Yes, but remember, Max didn't have to attract the majority of women in the community. He just needed to attract two—or maybe three, if there's one we haven't yet discovered."

Her husband nodded. "You have a point. What's the next step in your investigation?"

"Well, we still haven't identified Max's lady friend. I guess I'll get the name of the president of the Billiards Club and ask him about the women members of that club, the same way I did with regard to the YMC. You know, Dad said that Max avoided controversies while playing billiards; it was a peaceful refuge for him. So, in that setting, women may have found him more attractive."

Jeremy smiled. "I think the reason Sharon was able to find Max so attractive was that she met him during her first visit to the YMC, shortly after she moved to the community. She may never have had the chance to see Max's ugly side."

"Jerry, that's incredibly smart! That's downright profound!" Amy licked her lips and smiled devilishly. "You know what that does to me. I'm getting turned on again. We're going back for an immediate double-header!"

Jeremy had a terrified look on his face. In a plaintive voice, he cried out, "But Amy, I don't—"

"Poor, poor boy!" Amy interrupted, as she stroked her husband's cheek. "Don't you realize I'm just kidding?"

Jeremy breathed a sigh of relief. But he wasn't sure his wife had actually been kidding.

Wednesday, March 25, 2015, a.m.

At ten in the morning, Amy phoned Ralph, and he provided her with the name and phone number of the president of the Billiards Club.

At ten fifteen, Harry Packman answered his phone.

"Hello, Harry, this is Amy Bell."

"Ralph just phoned and told me to expect your call. Actually, I saw your presentation, and I was expecting you to contact me, as Max Gattner was a member of the Billiards Club. Have you made any progress in your investigation?"

"Well, I've made some progress, but nothing to get excited about. Everyone has to understand that the odds are against me solving the murder."

"Of course. I think we all do understand that, but we can hope."

"Harry, tell me about Max, based on your experiences with him."

"Sure. People have told me Max was very loud and unpleasant, but I only interacted with him in the context of the Billiards Club. He was friendly with all the members, and he was a courteous player who was gracious when he won as well as when he lost. He never raised his voice. He was a pretty good player, although there were several players who were quite a bit better. He sometimes gave suggestions to the less-skilled players—which they appreciated—to help improve their game."

Amy smiled. "You paint a picture of Max that is the complete opposite of the picture painted by many other residents."

Harry laughed. "Maybe our club members are so likeable that Max couldn't help but be on his best behavior with us!"

Now Amy laughed. "Hey, that's as good an explanation as any. I have another question. How many of the club members are women? Also, have any women quit the club in recent years, and are there any women who are nonmembers who show up?"

"There are only three women members; no one fits into your other two categories."

"For those three women, I'd like to know their approximate ages. Also, do any of them have husbands or significant others who are currently working?"

"Amy, I assume you can't tell me the reason why you ask."

She smiled and nodded. "No, I can't. I hope you understand."

"I figured as much. Two of the women are single; Marge Walcott is in her seventies, and so is Nancy Chaldor. They are both widows whose husbands died three or four years ago. I'm pretty sure they do not have significant others. Elaine Palletti has been married to Fred for a long time; they met in college. She is in her late fifties. Fred is a business executive; he runs the Southwestern US division of a British company."

"As part of his job, does he travel to England?"

"Interesting that you ask that. Elaine told me Fred flies to London for five days every month. The rest of the time, he works out of his company's office in Phoenix."

"Does Fred play billiards?"

"No, he never comes to the club, and Elaine told me he doesn't play."

"Do planes fly nonstop from Phoenix to London?"

"Yes, Elaine told me there are several airlines that fly nonstop."

"Wow," exclaimed Amy, "who'd have thunk it!"

Harry nodded. "Yeah, people—particularly those who live in the eastern half of our country—tend not to realize that Phoenix has truly become a world-class city."

Amy took down the contact information for all three women and thanked Harry for his assistance. She hung up and went over to her husband, who was working on his computer, and she gave him a big hug. "Jerry, I think we've found Max's lady friend. Her name is Elaine Palletti. She's in her late fifties, and her husband is in London on business five days every month. The rest of the time, he works in Phoenix. So she could have been with Max during the day and also several nights per month. She's the only married lady in the Billiards Club; actually, there are only three lady members."

Her husband nodded. "Sure looks like you've got her pegged. I take it you'll ask to interview Elaine at her house and check out her soap. If it's J'adore, will you then tell her you know all about her and Max?"

"That's a good question; I'm not sure what I'm gonna do. What do you think I should do?"

"Sweetheart, tell me the advantages and disadvantages of immediately confronting her."

"Well, the biggest disadvantage is that Elaine could become angry at me, terminate the conversation, and maybe also tell her husband that I falsely accused her. The advantage is that she may come clean and provide me with some useful information. Also, I only have another week here. I can't afford unnecessary delays in my investigation."

"What if Elaine found out about Sharon and killed Max for that reason? Then could there be a disadvantage if she finds out that you know about her and Max?"

"You're right; In that case, it might be better for me not to let on."

"Sweetheart, my guess is that you'll have to play it by ear. After speaking to her for awhile, you'll have a better feeling about how to handle it."

"You're right. But I'm still thinking about something we spoke about a few days ago. Why did the killer wait at least twenty-five minutes before going into the club room and murdering Max? So far, none of the possible explanations satisfy me. I think I'll phone Denise Bromfield and ask if she has any ideas. Then I'll call Cathy and Eddie. Eddie has been working the late shift recently, so he's probably home at this time." Amy picked up the phone and punched in Denise's number. "Denise is usually home on Wednesdays. And her husband, Gary, only goes in to his college two days a week this semester—what a racket!—so he could be home too."

Six years before, Denise was a beautiful and extremely intelligent twenty-seven-year-old waitress who never went to college but who loved to read books, particularly on business and economics. A very wealthy CEO who was twice her age met her when she served his table. He married her several weeks later. Three years into the marriage, the CEO died, and Denise inherited everything. She used her newfound wealth to set up and substantially fund a charity, Return to Learn. Amy met Denise while doing a murder investigation. They had since become very good friends. Amy had played a big role in getting Denise together with her current husband, Gary Bromfield, a college history professor. It was Gary who answered the phone.

"Hi, Amy. How's things?"

"We're in Arizona, celebrating my parents' forty-fifth anniversary. We won't be home for another week. What hot topic are you debating with Denise lately?"

"We've been discussing—all right, debating—what is the appropriate minimum wage."

Amy laughed. "Sounds right up Denise's alley. I'll bet she's thrashing you—I mean verbally."

Now Gary laughed. "It's more appropriate to say she's educating me, despite some resistance on my part."

"Gary, can you put her on? I have to ask her a question. It's okay to put her on speakerphone if you want to listen."

"Amy, I'll use this opportunity to go on the computer and look for evidence to back up my position regarding the minimum wage. Here she is."

Denise got on the phone. "Hello, Amy. When I heard Gary say it was you, I put on the speakerphone, so I've heard everything."

"You sneaky devil. I'll put on the speakerphone here for Jerry. How's your charity going?"

"Slowly but surely, we're gaining more contributors. I'm being invited to speak to quite a few civic organizations, which is more work for me, but great for the charity. So tell me your question."

"Believe it or not, I've been recruited into doing a murder investigation. As I said, I'm out here visiting my parents, and a resident of their community was smashed on the head with a baseball bat." Amy recounted the relevant details. "So do you have any ideas, other than the ones that have already been proposed, to explain the big time gap between Max entering the club room and the murder being committed?"

"Let me think." There was silence for about ten seconds. "Actually, I do have a possible explanation. You are assuming that the killer saw Max entering the club room at two forty-five. What if the killer did not see Max go in, but was a member of the Yankees/Mets Club who happened to be the first person to enter the club room for the film—not counting Max and not counting Ralph, who had already left. Say this person came into the club room at three twenty and saw Max alone, in the chair, napping. This person saw an opportunity and used the bat to kill Max. Then the killer left the club room and returned later, after other club members had already discovered Max's dead body."

"You know," Amy said, "that's very possible! I'm amazed that neither Jerry nor I, nor anyone else I spoke to, had thought of that. You are so damn smart! And I'm sure you didn't get that idea from any of the thousands of books you've read, so you came up with it all by yourself, in a matter of only a few seconds. Amazing!"

"Well, actually, I may have gotten the idea from a novel I read where—"

"Stop there," Amy interrupted, "I don't want to know!" She heard Denise and Gary laughing.

Amy got off the phone and looked at her husband. He was also quietly laughing. "*Et tu,* Jerry? Well, what do you think about Denise's idea?"

"Sweetheart, it's the best explanation we've heard so far for the time gap. But I have my own suggestion. I think it's very unlikely that Max's behavior in the YMC would cause someone to kill him. But if Denise is correct, then the killer is a member of the YMC. So I think you should be looking for members of the YMC who are also members of the Men's Discussion Group or who have had nasty exchanges with Max on the SDE Neighbors website."

Amy nodded. "I think you're right on target, even if Denise's idea is not correct, but even more so if it is correct. I am going to ask Mel to email me the names and contact information for all the members of the YMC, as well as the former members who quit because of Max. Then I can cross-check those names with the Men's Discussion Group and the SDE Neighbors website. But first, I'm phoning the Mitchells." She punched in their home phone number, and Cathy answered.

Cathy was, for the past decade, Amy's best girlfriend. For three and a half years, prior to Amy's marriage to Jeremy, she and Amy had been roommates. Eddie was now a detective in the NYPD, and he and Jeremy had known each other since grade school. So Amy and Jeremy considered the Mitchells to be like family. Fourteen months before, Cathy had given birth to her first child, a girl they named Aurora. Amy and Cathy both put on their speakerphones and spent a few minutes talking about Aurora. Then Amy recounted the details of the murder and asked the same question she'd given to Denise.

After a few seconds, Eddie spoke up. "Maybe while he was alone in the club room, Max phoned the killer, or maybe the killer phoned him, say at three fifteen. One or the other suggested that they should meet in person, for some reason. Max—who didn't realize the killer's intentions—suggested that the killer should come immediately to the club room, and mentioned that he was alone there. Then the killer went to the club room and murdered Max."

"That's a good idea, Eddie," Amy responded, "but we have the phone records. Max had no phone calls or texts after noon."

Now Cathy chimed in. "Maybe the killer saw Max go into the club room and followed him in. But at that time, the killer was not planning to murder Max. He or she just wanted to express some sort of grievance. But Max was nasty and maybe made some sort of insult or even a threat. The killer left, angry, at, say three o'clock, but after thinking for a while about what had just transpired, became even angrier and decided to kill Max. So the killer went back, at say three twenty, and did the deed."

"That makes some sense," Amy responded. "You may have nailed it. By the way, Eddie, I might possibly need your help to find out if certain people have criminal records."

Eddie was not surprised to hear this. Amy had requested his assistance several times in the past, and he had always done what he could to help her out. "No problem, Amy. Be sure to call us when you two get back to New York, so we can all get together."

Amy got off the phone and again looked at Jeremy. "So, what do you think?"

"I think that Cathy didn't nail it. If someone was going to kill Max on the spur of the moment, in a fit of rage because of nasty things Max said at their club room one-on-one meeting, the killing would be very likely to happen right after Max said those things, not twenty minutes later, when that person would be calmer and less prone to violence. But we can't completely rule out Cathy's idea."

Amy nodded. "I'm with you. Of course, there was no reason for me to say anything negative to Cathy about her idea. But one thing is for sure: there was a time gap, and there has to be a reason for it. I keep thinking I'm missing something very important."

"By the way, sweetheart, why would you ask Eddie to check out possible suspects when you have the deputy sheriff right here?"

"Because when I met with Alan, he made me feel very uncomfortable. I'd rather deal with him as infrequently as possible. But I'm not sure I'll actually need Eddie's help for this case.

"Now, Jerry, you're the actuary. Based on what we know, what's the probability that Elaine was Max's lady friend?"

Jeremy thought for a few seconds. "Well, I'll start by saying the probability is over ninety-five percent that Max did indeed have the kind of lady friend you're talking about. Now, given that he had a lady friend, if you find J'adore soap in Elaine's bathroom, it's nearly one hundred percent certain that she's the one. If you don't, the probability goes way down, I'd say to forty-five percent."

Amy was confused. "Where did you come up with that forty-five percent figure?"

Her husband laughed. "I'll come clean. I just made that number up out of thin air. Actually, if you don't find J'adore soap, I have no idea what the probability would then become."

Now Amy laughed. "Let's just hope I find the J'adore soap; I don't even want to think about the alternative."

Wednesday, March 25, 2015, p.m.

At two in the afternoon, Amy parked her car in the driveway of a house on Sunny Breeze Drive. It was larger than the other houses she'd previously visited. She figured it probably had three bedrooms, rather than two, and there was most likely a third bath.

She rang the bell and was let in by a five-foot-five woman with long brown hair, who was, in Amy's judgment, about fifteen pounds overweight, although still reasonably attractive. Elaine Palletti smiled as she shook Amy's hand. Amy felt the smile was forced. In fact, Elaine looked quite unhappy. Amy sat on a chair in the living room, while her hostess sat on the sofa. Elaine mentioned that her husband, Fred, was at work in Phoenix. Amy declined her offer of a drink.

"Elaine, as I said on the phone, given that Max Gattner was a member of the Billiards Club, I thought I should meet with each of the club members. But first, I have a kind of weird request." Amy repeated the same bathroom renovation story she had told to Wendy. And just like Wendy, Elaine laughed and led Amy to the master bath. Amy made a big show of inspecting the sinks, starting with the one which Elaine said she used. While complimenting the beauty of the granite sink counter, she saw a soap dish. There was a not-too-used bar of soap—whose shape and color she recognized—on the dish. She picked up the bar and briefly sniffed it. It was J'adore.

She proceeded to inspect Fred's sink, and then the two women returned to the living room. "So, Elaine, please tell me what you can about Max."

"Well," Elaine began, as her eyes alternated between looking at Amy and looking at the rug, "there's not too much I can say. I did sometimes play billiards with him during the Billiards Club hours— I had always called it pool. I was not a good player—actually that's an understatement. Sometimes, Max was kind enough to give me some pointers. I felt awful when I heard he was killed. That's about all I know." Now, Elaine was mainly looking at the rug. When Amy did not respond immediately, Elaine looked up at her guest. Elaine was no longer even attempting to smile. Amy thought she saw a look of hopelessness in the eyes of her hostess.

Amy knew what she should do. She went over to the sofa and sat down next to Elaine. She began to speak very softly. "Elaine, I'm a very good detective. So I know that you must have spent the last two months in misery, unable to tell anyone how you felt or why. You don't have to hide it from me; I know about you and Max."

Elaine immediately burst into tears. Amy hugged her for thirty seconds, as she moaned and wailed. Then Amy released the hug and took hold of Elaine's hand, a grip she maintained during the rest of their time on the sofa.

"How did you find out?"

"I wish I could tell you, but my methods and sources have to remain confidential. I hope you can understand."

"Do you know how long we were together?"

"My guess would be that it started in September or October of 2013."

"That's impossible; you couldn't know that!" Elaine had finally stopped crying and had succeeded in composing herself to some degree. "Are you being paid to investigate Max's murder?"

"No. My parents live in South Desert Estates, and I'm doing everything for free."

"Well, whatever they pay you in New York, it isn't enough. You're not just a detective; you must have super powers."

"You're very kind. Why don't you tell me the whole story?"

"It's such a relief to finally be able to talk to someone about this. You've actually freed me, in a way. Anyhow, Fred and I got married thirty-four years ago. We raised two children; we've been empty nesters for the past eight years. The feelings we initially had for each other diminished substantially over the years, but we were comfortable and content together—or so I thought.

"Four years ago, Fred was offered an executive position by Windsor Import/Export, which is a large British company with headquarters in London. He would be in charge of the Southwestern US office in Phoenix. This offer provided a substantial pay increase and lucrative stock options. Fred accepted the offer. I retired from my job as an Atlanta elementary school teacher, and we moved here to South Desert Estates.

"Fred knew when he took the job that he would periodically have to travel to London. There are nonstop flights from Phoenix to London, so it wasn't too much of a problem. During the first two and a half years, the pattern was that roughly every three months, he would travel to the UK for a three-day stay. Then he told me that he needed to go to London more often. He said it had been agreed that he would go to London, for a five-day period, during the second week of every month.

"This made no sense to me. Why did he have to be there in person so often, in this era of Skype and videoconferencing? I became more and more suspicious, so I found a detective agency with a branch in London, and I had Fred followed when he went there in September 2013. They discovered that he had a girlfriend in London, and he was spending every night there with her.

"I felt worthless and betrayed. But I didn't want to tell Fred what I knew, and I certainly did not want to get divorced. Being married provides great advantages and status, which can be even greater in a community such as this. We can socialize with other married couples for all sorts of activities, where a single, divorced lady would not fit in. Singles are often relegated to their own groups and activities. Of course we have all the clubs here at SDE, which anyone can join, but still it's much better to be married—at least that's how I feel.

"Anyhow, I was in emotional turmoil. I had joined the Billiards Club a few months before, and one afternoon, in late September, I went to the billiard room during their club hours. There were about ten people there. All four tables were in use. After a short wait, a table became available. I found myself playing a game of pool with Max. I'd seen him there before, but I had never really *noticed* him, if you know what I mean. He offered me a few tips to improve my game. I realized I was physically attracted to Max, and he seemed to be a nice guy.

"Prior to finding out that Fred was cheating, I certainly found some men attractive, but I never even dreamed of acting on those feelings. Now everything had changed. I made the first move. I smiled at Max and asked if we could get together in the billiard room at a different time, not during the club hours, where he could give me some more tips on how to improve my game. He agreed.

"When we got back together, the following morning, we were the only people in the billiard room. Max was in the process of giving me some advice when I grabbed him and kissed him on the lips. He seemed to enjoy it, and he asked me, 'Did you really mean that?' I said yes. He said, 'Aren't you married?' I said, 'Yes. But it is no longer a happy marriage, and my husband has a girlfriend.' Max then pulled me close and kissed me passionately. We took it from there.

"Of course, no one could know. We agreed that if one of us wanted to phone the other, that person would use the free clubhouse phone to make the call. There would be no emails or texts. At first, Max and I would drive our cars—Fred has his own car which he drives to work in Phoenix—to an isolated location a few miles from SDE, and we would neck, or whatever, in one of the cars. But Max soon took steps to enable us to safely go to his house.

"He traded in his old car and bought a new Honda Accord. He had it fitted with a privacy divider between the front and the back, as well as privacy windows in the back. Then here's what we did to avoid detection—"

Amy couldn't control herself. She interrupted and took a shot. "Did it involve Walmart?"

"Amy, you are either a superhero, a sorceress, or a witch. There is no possible way you could have acquired that information."

Amy smiled. "Actually, I was just making an educated guess."

Elaine laughed. "Okay, maybe you're not a witch. Anyhow, as you have apparently deduced, we would drive our cars to the Walmart lot and park there. I would get into the back seat of Max's car, where nobody could see me, and we drove back to Max's house, and into his garage, from which we entered his house. Twice a week, I spent three or four hours during the day with Max at his house while

Fred was at work in Phoenix. When Fred was in London for five days, I spent two or three nights at Max's house."

"Elaine, did you and Max have any sort of understanding regarding exclusivity? Could either of you see other people?"

"How could I demand exclusivity of Max while I was married to Fred? I always told him there were no strings to our relationship. When we were not together, he—and I—could do whatever we pleased. Obviously, for me, things were complicated enough as it was, so there was no way I was going to be involved with a third man. It would have been easier for Max, but as far as I am aware, he wasn't seeing any other women.

"You should know that I connected with Max on a much deeper level than I'd ever had with Fred, or at least much deeper than I'd had with him after the first few years of our marriage. And you're right—the past two months have been sheer misery for me. I feel such a sense of relief now that I've told it all to you. But I don't know what I'm going to do with my life from here on, to have a chance for some happiness.

"And Amy, I'm asking you to keep what I've just told you as confidential as possible."

Amy nodded. "Other than my husband, who helps me with my cases, I've told no one what I found out about you and Max. I hope I never have to tell anyone, and I will make every effort to that end, but I can't make an ironclad promise."

Now Elaine nodded. "I understand. I know you're trying to solve a murder. But I'm trusting you, as a superhero, to do everything you reasonably can to try to keep it confidential."

"Isn't the proper word *superheroine*?" asked Amy. They both laughed.

Amy continued, "What were you and Fred doing on the afternoon of the murder?"

"We were mingling, separately, at the club event in the social hall. We drove there together, in Fred's car, at about one forty-five. We agreed to meet back at the car at three forty-five. I got there a minute or so before Fred. We knew we had to get home promptly, so that we could get ready to leave at five for dinner at a local restaurant with two other SDE couples. As I was leaving the clubhouse to meet Fred, I saw some sort of ruckus going on down the hall, but because of the time pressure, I didn't check it out. I didn't find out about Max being killed until the next day."

"I assume you're confident that Fred never found out about you and Max."

"I'm very confident that he has never found out, just as I'm equally confident that Fred doesn't know that I am aware of his girlfriend in London."

"I'm sure you know that Max created a lot of controversy in the community."

Elaine smiled. "That's a very gentle way of putting it. Max was from Queens, New York. So he was not a Southern gentleman. He was a strong and spirited advocate of his opinions, and he didn't hold back when he thought people were ignorant or fools. I think he greatly enjoyed all his verbal combat. He certainly wasn't trying to hurt anyone, even if people sometimes wrongly interpreted his words in that way. I understood him, and knowing that he cared so strongly about things and forcefully defended his views made me love him even more."

"Elaine, did Max ever mention the names of any people who he was worried might want to do him physical harm?"

"No, Max never said he was worried about physical violence, and he certainly never mentioned any names. I believe Max thought most of the people with whom he verbally sparred actually enjoyed it as much as he did. And to this day, I still find it hard to believe that any of those people would kill Max.

"Amy, as I said, I don't know what to do with my life at this point. Can you give me some advice? I can't ask this question to anyone else but you, as you are the only one who knows the whole story."

Amy was silent for about ten seconds before responding. "I have a reputation for liking to give people advice—sometimes solicited and sometimes unsolicited. I wish so badly that I had some perceptive and helpful advice I could provide to you, but I'm not able to do that, at least not at this point. However, I will always be available—here or in New York—for you to phone me, whenever you feel the need."

The two women hugged, and Amy departed. At three o'clock, she arrived back at the hotel and related to Jeremy her interview with Elaine. "I'm sure I did the right thing by telling Elaine I knew about her and Max."

"Sweetheart, you are acting like you are also sure that Elaine did not kill Max. Am I right?"

Amy nodded. "You're right. I'm almost certain she didn't do it."

"Well, let me tell you why I think you shouldn't be so sure. As I see it, there are two big general questions in this case. The first is how to account for the gap between the time the killer observed Max entering the club room and the time of the murder. We have extensively discussed this question. You have also asked Denise, Cathy, and Eddie—and even the deputy sheriff—if they could come up with an explanation.

"The second question has come up before, but we put it aside and didn't spend too much time discussing it. And that's why, after years of Max being a loudmouth boor, did someone suddenly decide to kill him on January 31?

"Obviously, the logical answer is that the situation changed for the killer, with regard to Max, on or shortly before January 31. And one person who fits that bill is Elaine. She told you she didn't think Max was seeing any other women. She also said there were no strings. But what if she lied? What if she found out about Max and Sharon cavorting around in an amorous way? Or maybe she even found out that he went to Sharon's house with her. This was only a few days prior to January 31. She became enraged; she had been betrayed for a second time. So she murdered Max. This scenario doesn't preclude her being miserable for the past two months. Of course, she now realizes that—even only considering her best interest—she made a terrible mistake by killing Max.

"I know you feel there can be a long-term buildup of insults from Max that may have reached critical mass for the killer on January 31. But, for me, that theory doesn't ring true."

Amy smiled. "Jerry, you've really been thinking about this! Couldn't Fred also fit your criterion? What if, shortly before January 31, he found out about his wife and Max? She says he still doesn't know, but maybe—just like his wife—he hired a detective, who found out everything and recently told him."

Jeremy nodded. "Yeah, that's also possible, but I think it's less likely."

"On the contrary, Jerry, I think that given all the circumstances—and assuming they both found out what was going on—Fred would be much more likely than Elaine to murder Max. But the best evidence is that neither of them know anything. Elaine doesn't know about Sharon, and Fred doesn't know about Max. In that case, we don't yet have a good answer to your second question."

"Why don't you call Eddie and ask if he can find out if Fred has a criminal record—any evidence of past violent behavior?"

"You know, Jerry, I think I will. And I'll also give him Elaine's name. But I'm pretty sure they'll both come up with clean slates. And, as you suggested, that will leave us with two critical questions, both without satisfying answers—at least as far as I'm concerned. This only reinforces my feeling—which I've previously expressed to you—that I'm missing something really significant."

"So, sweetheart, what is your next step, besides calling Eddie?"

"It's time to look at those SDE Neighbors postings. Let's see who Max was having it out with there. Then I'll have to check into the Men's Discussion Group."

At this point, Amy's phone rang. It was Cathy. "Amy, I have another possible explanation for the time gap. The killer saw Max enter the club room but wasn't thinking of killing him at that time. However, a few minutes later, someone told the killer about some horrible thing that Max had said or done. This was the last straw for the killer, who realized that Max may be alone in the club room, which would be a good opportunity to kill him. This was at, say, three twenty. Max was indeed still alone, and the killer murdered him."

Amy profusely thanked her best girlfriend and hung up. She told her husband what Cathy had said. He smiled. "You have to give her credit for trying to help you out. She's certainly going the extra mile."

Amy nodded. "True. For what it's worth, Denise's suggestion is still the best of a shabby lot, in my opinion. But I have to get to that SDE Neighbors website! And also I have to call Mel." Amy punched in the number. "Hi, Mel, can you email me the names and contact information for all the YMC members, plus the men who quit the club because of Max?"

"Sure, Amy, I'll send the list right out to you, as an attachment."

"By the way, do you know if any of these people are also in the Men's Discussion Group?"

"I know that Richard Garmin attends the Men's Discussion Group. Offhand, I am not aware of any others."

Amy thanked Mel, got off the phone, and then picked up the massive SDE Neighbors printout she had received from the deputy sheriff. Jeremy went back to his work on the computer, grateful that Amy had not requested his assistance with the printout.

After several hours of reading postings—broken up by dinner at an Italian restaurant—Amy told her husband what she had determined. "Jerry, this guy Max was vile! Other people can tell you he was a nasty boor, but you have to actually read what he posted to understand the true depth of his disgustingness."

Her husband laughed. "Sweetheart, I wish you wouldn't hold back your feelings; tell me what you really think about Max!"

Now Amy burst into hysterical laughter. It took her a while to calm down.

"Jerry, I want you to read a page or two, just to get an idea of what I'm talking about."

Jeremy followed instructions and then declared, "Max was even worse than I had imagined."

"See, I told you so! But there are two men, Aaron Wallman and Ray Luddell, who are the most likely suspects from the bunch of people Max insulted. During the two-month period of website postings that Alan sent me, they posted back and forth with Max over a hundred times each, hurling epithets at Max in response to his epithets. The other people who Max insulted posted only once or twice—or at most three times—and generally didn't bother responding to Max.

"And they were usually fighting over the stupidest things, such as whether the community's holiday season decorations were appropriate or how many parking spots in the clubhouse lot should be reserved for golf carts.

"Oh, and there's a third person, Fern Maybrook. Max posted, on January 29, that she had seriously violated the SDE bylaws, and he was going to report her. He said Ms. Maybrook would face severe repercussions, and she would live to regret what she had done."

"Sweetheart, what had this lady done?"

"Max didn't say, and the lady never posted a response. Actually, I didn't see any postings from Fern. By the way, I got the YMC list from Mel, and nobody on that list had posted on the SDE Neighbors website during the two months of postings that Alan sent me."

"Well, it's good that you cross-checked. But based on what you've told me, Fern Maybrook is your most likely suspect. I'd say people don't kill each other over epithets on websites. But when someone threatens a homeowner with severe repercussions, I can imagine the homeowner using violence to squelch the threat."

"But Jerry, once Max publicized on the website that Fern had violated the bylaws, the cat was out of the bag. The board would become cognizant that there was an issue. Somebody would investigate what was going on. Max being dead would probably not make much of a difference for Fern."

"Yes, but as you have said, some women may not be that rational. This was particularly true in the days right after Max made his threat. And Max was murdered two days after his threat was posted."

"Well, I'm going to try to interview all three of them tomorrow. And depending on how those interviews go, I may ask Eddie to check them out."

"Do you have any gut feelings yet, regarding this case?"

Amy smiled. "Not in the way you mean, but with this case, I do have the feeling that I will be like Potter Stewart."

"Potter who?"

"Potter Stewart. He was a justice on the Supreme Court. He is famous for writing that while he can't define pornography, he knows it when he sees it. My gut says I'll know who the killer is when I meet and interview him—or her. But Lord only knows how I'll be able to prove that person is the killer."

"Why do you think you'll be able to recognize the killer?"

"I have no logical reason. It's just a feeling. And there's something else I'm feeling right now." She flashed a sexy smile at her husband and licked her lips. Jeremy knew what feeling his wife was now referring to, and he responded accordingly.

Thursday, March 26, 2015, a.m.

At ten in the morning, Aaron Wallman offered Amy Bell a chair in his dining room. He was five feet eleven and appeared to be in excellent shape. Amy knew he was sixty years old, retired, and divorced.

"Aaron, do you work out a lot in the gym?"

"Yes, I'm there for over an hour every morning."

Amy smiled. "I could tell. As we discussed on the phone, I'm investigating the killing of Max Gattner."

"Actually, Amy, I was at your presentation in the social hall. You did a first-rate job up there. It was very impressive, very interesting."

"Thank you. Did anyone from the sheriff's office speak to you?"

"Yes, for about three minutes. I told the guy I knew nothing about the murder, and he gave me his card and said to call if I come up with anything that could help their investigation."

How wonderfully thorough! Amy thought. "Aaron, I'd like you to tell me everything you can about Max. I know you two had disputes on the SDE Neighbors website."

"Actually, my only interaction with Max was on that website. I knew what he looked like—and I assume he knew what I looked like—but on the occasions when I noticed him at the clubhouse, I made sure not to go near him, make eye contact, or speak to him. He was an ugly man—and not just physically.

"I care about this community. I frequently post on the SDE Neighbors website, in an effort to comment on things that are going on here and to make suggestions for improvement. Other people also post their observations and suggestions. We learn from each other. Except for Max. He would respond to my postings by calling me a jerk, an idiot, or worse."

Amy smiled. "You called Max a few names too."

"Yes, but that was after he started it. I would make a posting on a topic and maybe get into a conversation on the website with some other people regarding my posting. Then Max would chime in with his insults. When someone hits me, I hit back. If he hits me a second time, I hit back a second time. I think you get the picture."

Amy smiled. "Yes, I do."

"You're from New York City, right?"

"That's right. I've lived there my whole life."

"Well, Max was from New York City, and he was the embodiment of all the horrible stereotypes people from the rest of the country have about your city. I've been to New York several times, so I know most New Yorkers are good, decent people. But most folks haven't been there. So, frankly, people like you, who live in New York, should be particularly grateful that Max is dead."

"Were you at the club event at the social hall on the afternoon Max was murdered?"

"Yes, I hung out there for about an hour, between two and three, and then I went home. But of course, at this point, I can't prove anything. I'm sure that with everyone milling around, virtually no one who was there can prove anything."

Amy nodded. "You're probably right about that."

"Well, there's one thing I'll say that every other man you interview will confirm. You are one hell of a good-looking, well-built detective!"

Amy turned beet red. "Thank you for the compliment."

"Actually, the other men you speak to might not come out and confirm what I said, but they'll all be thinking it. Be sure to tell your husband what I've just told you."

"I'll tell him. And, Aaron, as I said before, you're in pretty good shape yourself."

Amy departed and headed for her next appointment. At ten forty-five, she was greeted at the front door by a hefty five-foot-eight woman in her early sixties, with what Amy figured was well-dyed, dark brown hair. She told Amy she was Roberta Luddell. "Let's all go into the living room; Ray is already there."

Roberta directed Amy to a chair and instructed her husband to move over to a different chair from the one he had been sitting in. Roberta then sat down between them, so that Amy's view of Ray was partially obstructed. He looked about ten years older than his wife, despite Amy knowing he was actually only sixty-four. He was also a couple of inches shorter than Roberta.

It's obvious who is the head of household here! Amy chuckled to herself, as she declined Roberta's offer of a drink. Amy was ready to speak, but Roberta beat her to the punch. "Amy, we are so sorry we couldn't get to see your presentation. We tried to sign up the day before, but the event was already filled to capacity. And people told me you were so interesting!"

"Well, thank you so much, Roberta, for saying that. I'm sorry that—"

"So," Roberta interrupted, "of course Ray and I want to help you out as much as possible with your investigation."

"That's right," said Ray. "Let me start with the SDE Neighbors website. I would say—"

"Yes, Amy," Roberta interjected, "the deputy from the sheriff's office came and asked Ray about the website. I told him what I'm now telling you. Ray retired from a very active career as a business executive. Now that he and I are here, there are clubs and all, but I'd say Ray has been a bit restless—you know, looking for satisfying activities.

"It turns out that posting on the SDE Neighbors website is very satisfying for Ray. He does it with great frequency, having conversations with other SDE residents on a variety of topics. But what provided Ray with the most pleasure and satisfaction was his verbal combat with Max Gattner. Ray would make a posting and tell me he hoped Max would respond with his usual stupidity, so that he could sock it back to Max. Ray would read me the response he planned to send to Max, and he would ask me if I thought it should be modified in any way. This stuff was the highlight of his day. Right, honey?"

Ray nodded. "You're right, dear. I felt—"

"So," Roberta continued, "for Ray, selfishly speaking, Max's death has been quite a blow."

"Roberta," Amy inquired, now knowing for sure to whom questions should be directed, "about how long was your conversation with the deputy sheriff?"

"He was here for less than five minutes. He gave me his card, with his number on it, in case we thought of something else he should know."

"Can you tell me where the two of you were on the afternoon of Max's killing?"

"Yes, Ray and I went together to the clubhouse for the club event in the social hall. We were there from one thirty till three, roughly speaking. We were together the whole time, and we went home together. Right, honey?"

"Yes, dear, that's right."

At least she let him finish that four-word sentence! Amy thought. "Did either of you see Max there?"

"Well," Ray responded, "I—"

"Absolutely not!" Roberta chimed in. "Neither of us saw Max on the day he was killed, in the social hall or anywhere else. I also mentioned that to the deputy sheriff."

Roberta let Ray shake hands with Amy; then she led Amy to the front door and shook Amy's hand before Amy exited. She was back at the hotel by eleven forty.

She kissed her husband. "Jerry, did you tell me you have a tennis date for this afternoon?"

"Yes, at one thirty. I was going to take a taxi."

"I have a better idea. Get your tennis clothes on now. I'll drive us to the SDE clubhouse, where we can eat lunch at the café. Then I'll take you over to the tennis courts. When I'm finished interviewing Fern, I'll head back to the court and watch you finish your match. Then I'll drive us home. By the way, you will be wearing your tennis shorts, right?"

"Yes."

"Good! So, while I'm observing your match, I'll be able to watch something much more interesting than the tennis ball, namely your sexy legs."

Thursday, March 26, 2015, p.m.

Over lunch at the clubhouse café, Amy told her husband about her two morning interviews. "So Aaron says I'm good-looking and well-built."

"Well, sweetheart, of course he's right. I'm surprised none of the other men you've spoken to has said similar stuff to you. Of course, Ray wouldn't tell you you're good-looking unless his wife instructed him to do so."

Amy burst into laughter. "You know, Jerry, we can be amused by Roberta stopping her husband from talking, but there are two possible explanations for that which are deadly serious. First, she may know or suspect that he killed Max, and she thinks he'll trip up if she lets him answer my questions. Roberta is Ray's alibi. Of course, a suspect's wife is not the best alibi. But in this case, it's a better alibi than most of our suspects have, due to the nature of the club event in the social hall.

"Then there's the second possible explanation. Roberta herself may have killed Max, because of the way he insulted her husband, and maybe for some additional reasons we are not aware of. She's a big, probably strong woman. In this scenario, Ray is her alibi."

"So," Jeremy chimed in, "you're saying their story, that Ray enjoyed trading insults with Max, could well be a fabrication."

"That's exactly right. Not everyone enjoys being called a stupid pig."

"Did Max actually use those words on the website?"

"Yes, he did, and that wasn't the worst thing he called Ray. I think I'll ask Eddie to check out Aaron, Ray, and Roberta. I'll also throw in Fern. She's a widow, with no apparent significant other, so she probably doesn't have someone ready to lie to give her an alibi for the time of the murder. Anyhow, I'm interested in hearing what she has to say."

At one thirty, Amy arrived at the home of Fern Maybrook. It was on Panorama Lane, eight houses down from where Max had lived. There was a handwritten note taped to the front door: "Dear Amy, I'm jogging. Be back soon."

Ten minutes later, Amy observed a woman jogging down the street, at a pretty decent pace, toward where she was standing. Fern stopped in front of Amy, smiled, said hello, and opened the front door. Amy was directed to a chair in the dining room. Fern headed to the bathroom to wash up. Five minutes later, she sat down next to Amy. Fern had short gray hair and a confident look. Amy knew she was sixty-one years old.

Fern immediately began to speak. "Amy, I was wondering if and when you would contact me. I was at your presentation. It was by far the most interesting one in the three years I've lived here—and I've been to all of them. By the way, you have one hell of a hunky husband. I trust you know how to make sure he sticks around."

Amy laughed. "Yes, I know how. I'll tell Jerry you find him hunky; he'll be pleased."

"Anyhow, I decided that if you did not contact me, then you weren't as good a detective as we were led to believe. But here you are. So maybe you're an even better detective than we thought."

Amy laughed. "Fern, did the sheriff's office contact you?"

"No, they didn't. But let me tell you what I would have told them. You are here because of Max's posting on the SDE Neighbors website, right?"

"Right."

"Okay, I don't visit that website, so I didn't know about Max's posting regarding me until a few days after Max was killed. A friend in the community told me about it. Apparently he threatened to report me for violating the SDE bylaws.

"Well, I walk my next-door neighbor's dog, Trixie, when he can't be around to walk her. He reciprocates by troubleshooting when I have problems with my computer.

"Anyhow, there was an occasion—I think it was the Wednesday before Max died—when the dog defecated on Max's front area, just off the sidewalk. It's not like I wanted this to happen. But for some reason, Trixie suddenly lunged onto Max's property as we walked on the sidewalk past his house. And before I could take corrective action, she did her deed. Of course I carried a plastic bag, and I cleaned it up. But Max was home and saw the whole thing. He came out of the house and shouted at me. And I never walked Trixie past Max's house again—we took another route. But I'm sure that incident was what Max was referring to on the website.

"Max and I had never spoken to each other—except possibly to say hello when we passed each other on the street—before this happened. The friend who told me about Max's posting told me that Max was a total nut, and no one took him seriously. Since then, I've asked a few other people about Max, and they have all confirmed what my friend said. Still, nobody had the right to murder him. I hope you succeed in identifying the killer."

"Fern, did anyone else observe Trixie's indiscretion and Max shouting at you?"

"Not to my knowledge."

"Do you have any children or a significant other?"

"No. I didn't marry until I was forty-one. Jack died two years ago. I'm open to meeting another man, but there's been nothing like that so far."

"Where were you on the afternoon of the murder?

"I was in the social hall for the club event, between about one fifteen and three thirty. I had jogged there from my house, and I jogged home. Lots of people saw me in the social hall. I visited most of the club desks."

Amy thanked Fern for meeting with her, and she departed and proceeded to the tennis courts. She always enjoyed watching her husband run back and forth in his tennis outfit. When Jeremy finished his match at three fifteen, he walked over and kissed his wife.

"Fern says you're one hell of a hunky husband. And I second that."

"Did you enjoy watching the match? I guess you realize I got beat again."

Amy smiled. "Let's just say I enjoyed watching; never mind the match." Jeremy laughed.

When they got back to the hotel, Amy related her conversation with Fern. "She's athletic; she could easily have swung that bat down on Max. And we only have her word for it that Max was referring to dog poop. It could have been something much more serious."

"That's all true," Jeremy said, "but I now have to disagree with something you previously said. You thought that once Max had posted, the cat was out of the bag, and his death wouldn't help Fern too much. But as Fern's friend told her, people didn't take Max seriously. It is likely that with Max dead, no one on the board—or anyone else, for that matter—would pursue his assertion that Fern had seriously violated the bylaws."

Amy nodded. "You're right. What I said was not correct. If Fern was doing something really bad—and a canine indiscretion doesn't qualify—then she had a motive to kill Max. She claimed she didn't know about Max's posting until after he was dead, but she may be lying. And I may also have to take back what I said about my gut feeling that I'll know the killer when I interview them. I have to admit that with Roberta, Ray, and Fern, my gut has gone on vacation."

"Sweetheart, I'm going to repeat my gut feeling and remind you that boorish jerks are everywhere, particularly—I suspect—in places like this. People dislike them, avoid them, and don't take them seriously. But people don't suddenly decide to murder them on January 31. And unless Fern's violation of the bylaws is something like cocaine dealing, she's in the same category.

"However, recently discovering that your spouse or significant other is cheating is a different matter. People have been known to commit murder in that situation. So Elaine and Fred are my prime suspects, although you may say that it's unlikely they discovered anything—and that Elaine told you there were no strings with Max, and Fred had a girlfriend in London."

Amy nodded. "Point noted." She punched in the phone number for Ralph. "Hi Ralph, this is Amy Bell. Who do I have to contact to get the membership list for the Men's Discussion Group?"

"It's not actually a club, so they don't have official members. There's a coordinator, Nicholas Razar, who arranges with the clubhouse staff to have a room available and post the dates and times for meetings on the clubhouse bulletin boards and in the emails sent to the residents. Nicholas also serves as moderator for the group. He suggests topics and recognizes speakers. He has told me that he prefers to maintain a nonpartisan role and not provide his own views on any issue. I think there is an attendance sheet for every group meeting, so Nicholas may be able to provide you with the names from some of those sheets. I'll get you his phone number and email. I'll also call him right now and tell him to expect your call, so wait ten minutes before you phone him."

Ralph provided the contact information. Amy hung up, waited fifteen minutes, and phoned Nicholas. "Hello, Amy. Ralph just called me and said you'd like the names from the attendance sheets. I have them from January through now. I can scan the sheets you want and send them to you as an attachment to an email."

"Great, I really appreciate it. All I need are the sheets from January. May I just read you the names of the Yankees/Mets Club members and ask if you recognize any of them as having attended your group meetings?"

"Sure, go ahead."

Amy read off the names.

"The only one I recognize as being in our group is Richard Garmin. He's a regular with us. I know you're investigating Max's murder, so I guess you'd like to hear my input, right?"

"Yep, that was going to be my next question."

"Well, we discuss a lot of politics, and Max was on the far left, if you know what I mean. Trouble is, he was completely intolerant of differing opinions. For example, someone would speak in opposition to affirmative action, and Max's response would be, 'You must be close and cozy with the Klan!' Actually, that was his favorite response to people who disagreed with him on a whole bunch of issues. But he did have other responses, such as 'Heil Hitler'."

"Oh, my God! Max actually said that?"

"More than once."

"Nicholas, when you tell me this, I'm taken back to my own past. I'm very liberal politically. I used to be intolerant and call people names if they were conservative. Of course, I don't think I was ever as off the wall as Max was, but I'm ashamed of the way I acted. Then I met my future husband, Jeremy. He's an admirer of Ronald Reagan. Being with him made me realize that good people can have different political views than I do. That's just one of so many great things that being married to Jerry has done for me. I'm sorry; I'm going on and on."

Nicholas nodded. "I can understand what you're saying; Maureen has been a big positive influence on me, in many ways."

"Are there any people who had particularly bad disputes with Max in the weeks before he was killed?"

"Yes, there are two guys who stand out. During January, both nearly came to blows with Max—on separate occasions during group meetings. On both occasions, another man and I got up and separated them before anyone actually landed a punch.

"By the way, after Max was killed, our group adopted a rule that personal insults are prohibited and can result in suspension of the right to attend meetings. Frankly, we should have adopted this rule a long time ago."

"Do you have the names and contact information for the two men?"

"Sure. Wendell Samet and Carl Robbins. I'll look up their contact info. And I'll also email you the attendance sheets."

Nicholas provided the information, and Amy thanked him and got off the phone. She smiled at her husband. "Jerry, I have the names of two people in the Men's Discussion Group who would have come to blows with Max if other people hadn't separated them. Will you agree that they are prime suspects?"

"Sorry, sweetheart, but I don't agree. Sure, they might want to hit Max after he calls them whatever, but that's an immediate reaction, far different from murdering Max at a later time."

"Even if he called them Hitler and said they were cozy with the Klan?"

Jeremy nodded. "Right, even if he called them Hitler and said they were cozy with the Klan."

"Well, I'm hoping that I can interview those two men tomorrow and also Richard Garmin, who seems to be the only person in both the YMC and the Men's Discussion Group." Amy immediately started making phone calls. She was done at four forty-five.

"Jerry, I have an interview with Richard at seven o'clock this evening at the clubhouse café, and I'll meet with Wendell and Carl tomorrow morning at their homes."

"I'm amazed that everyone you've asked for an interview has readily agreed to meet with you."

"Actually, you shouldn't be surprised. People I ask for an interview realize that if they refuse, I will not keep that fact a secret, and their friends and neighbors in the community are apt to find out. They'll be under a cloud of suspicion."

Jeremy nodded. "You're right; I hadn't thought about it that way. Yes, if I lived here, I'd be afraid not to talk to you. I might not tell you the truth, but I would definitely meet with you. So let's eat dinner together at the clubhouse café. Then, when Richard shows up, I'll go to the gym and use the treadmill until you come and get me."

"Okay, sounds like a plan."

While they were eating dinner in the café, Amy's phone rang. "Amy," her father said, "I feel very guilty imposing on you again, but one of my really good friends here, Pete Sandover, approached me regarding a problem he has. It's a problem regarding the stock market, but it's not like he wants financial advice. He asked me to see if you would let him tell you about his situation and then give him your feedback. He saw your presentation and said he would also like Jeremy to be there. He's a widower with no children; he's as close to Carole and me as he is to anyone."

"Dad, did he go over his problem with you?"

"Sort of, but he knows I have nothing but contempt for Wall Street. And from what he did say, I couldn't give him any help. Can you and Jeremy come over here at one thirty tomorrow and let him explain what's going on? If you two hear him out and then feel unqualified to provide any advice, Pete will absolutely understand."

Amy sighed. "Okay, Dad, Jeremy and I will see you at your house at one thirty tomorrow. But please promise me that you won't find any other friends who need advice."

Irving laughed. "That's a promise. Thank you, and also thank Jeremy for me."

Amy got off the phone and smiled at her husband. "Tomorrow afternoon, you and I get to play problem solver for one of my father's friends. His name is Pete Sandover. It has something to do with the stock market, but it's not financial advice. Pete specifically asked for both of us."

"You know, sweetheart, this is the first time I'll be working on a case with you, right from the start as an equal partner. I'm actually looking forward to this! And I wish you'd stop staring at me—up and down. We're in public."

"Jerry, I can't help it; you look so sexy in your exercise outfit."

Richard Garmin showed up at six fifty-five, and Jeremy departed for the gym. "Amy, I was expecting you to contact me, as I was with Max in both the YMC and the Men's Discussion Group."

"Tell me about how you and Max interacted."

"Well, Max had one favorite word when addressing me, and that word was 'sucker.' The way he pronounced it, he stretched out the syllables and raised his tone at the end, like this: suuhh-kerr! In the Men's Discussion Group, for example, if I said something he disagreed with, like 'the policeman in Ferguson did nothing wrong in the Michael Brown case,' for example, Max would respond, 'You actually believe that? Suuhh-kerr!' Of course what he called me was mild compared to what he called some other people. That may be because he knew he'd also be seeing me in the YMC.

"And talking about the YMC, I think I actually was a bit of a sucker. He got me to bet him a few times regarding baseball trivia. Thinking about it, I'm sure he looked the stuff up on the Internet before bringing it up to me and goading me into making a bet. And when I paid off the bet, he would yell it out, so the other club members could hear: 'Suuhh-kerr!'

"But he was so outrageous that I found him funny. I actually looked forward to seeing Max in action. I saw some other people at the Men's Discussion Group smiling broadly when Max spouted off. I think Max also was their entertainment. But of course, not everyone there felt that way."

Amy chimed in, "So some people got very angry at Max; anyone in particular?"

"Well, the one who clearly comes to mind is Carl Robbins. We had a Men's Discussion Group meeting in early January, and he nearly got into a fistfight with Max, right in front of the club members. Some of our people had to step in to break them up. A couple of days later, I ran into Carl, and he told me that as long as Max was there, he wouldn't be attending any more meetings of the Men's Discussion Group. Carl did return to the group after Max was killed."

"Is there anyone else who got physical with Max or who seemed to you like he might want to?"

"No one else comes to mind. But I did miss two meetings in January, so something could have happened then that I am not aware of."

"Where were you on the afternoon of the murder?"

Richard laughed. "Where everybody else was—at the club event in the social hall. I actually saw Max there. I stayed from start to finish, going from table to table and engaging in small talk with some new residents. Yes, I did leave the social hall, probably twice, to go to the men's room. No, I can't prove where I was at the time when Max was killed. It was at about three twenty or so, right?"

"Yes, you're right."

"Then, at three forty-five, I went to the club room for the YMC movie, and I discovered that Max had been killed."

Amy thanked Richard, and then she went to the gym to get her husband. She stared at him from behind for a few minutes as he ran on the treadmill before making her presence known. Then they drove back to the hotel, where she related her interview to him. "So Richard claims he basically found Max amusing and looked forward to observing his antics. And he claims several other members of the Men's Discussion Group felt the same way."

Jeremy smiled. "That's no surprise to me. As a matter of fact, given how totally beyond the bounds Max was, I probably would have felt the same way as Richard."

"Well, tomorrow morning, I'll interview two people who were not amused. And I view them as serious suspects, particularly Carl Robbins. After all, if he wasn't coming back to the group as long as Max was there, killing Max was a way to make sure Max wasn't ever gonna show up again."

Friday, March 27, 2015, a.m.

At 9:25 a.m., Amy received a call from Eddie. "Amy, none of the people you asked me to check out has any kind of police record." Amy wasn't really surprised; she thanked Eddie and hung up.

At ten fifteen, Amy parked her car in the driveway of a house on Silver Sky Drive. She rang the bell and was greeted by Wendell Samet. Amy noted that her host was about five feet eight and quite overweight—actually the proper word would be fat. She knew he was a widower and that he was sixty-eight years old. They sat in the dining room. Amy accepted a Diet Coke.

"Amy, I know why you're visiting me, and…oh, wow! Do detectives actually look like you? If I knew you looked like this, I would have made it a point to attend your presentation!"

Amy smiled. "I appreciate the compliment. And I'm here to get your take on your dispute with Max, in the Men's Discussion Group this past January."

"Well, Amy, my take is that I'm absolutely ashamed of myself. Max was mentally ill; everyone in this community who interacted with him knew that. That includes everyone who ever heard Max at the Men's Discussion Group. When someone is ill, like Max was, the proper thing to do is to just let him act out, and to feel sorry for him. That's the way I responded to Max, as a general rule. But on that one occasion, in January, I strayed. Yes, I strayed."

"*Lovers and Other Strangers*," Amy interrupted with a smile.

"What?"

"Oh, I'm sorry. I was thinking about a movie. You were saying that you strayed."

"Right. On that day, I was speaking at the Men's Discussion Group; I said that with rare exceptions, the police enforce the law impartially and are not racist. Max responded by giving me the Nazi salute and saying 'Heil Hitler.' You can't tell from my name, but I'm Jewish. I have relatives who died at Auschwitz. I lost control, and I charged at Max. Luckily, two men stopped me."

Amy nodded. "I'm Jewish too, so I can understand how you felt."

"I'm glad you understand, but that doesn't excuse my behavior. I actually phoned Max the next day and apologized. He said he accepted my apology. We had one more group meeting before Max was killed. At that meeting, Max actually controlled himself with regard to me, although he spouted off against some other people."

"Wendell, where were you on the afternoon of the murder?"

"Jay Allton and I were manning the Men's Discussion Group desk at the club event in the social hall."

"I assume you took breaks, to use the men's room and to mingle."

"Occasionally, but only for a few minutes at a time."

Amy thanked Wendell for his time and departed. Her next stop was on the same street, twelve houses down. A petite, attractive woman in her fifties opened the door and introduced herself as Amanda Robbins. Amy was led to the living room, where Carl joined the two women. He was five foot seven and appeared to be in excellent shape. Amy knew he was sixty-two years old. Amy declined an offer of a drink. Remembering her interview with Ray, Amy wondered if Carl's wife was going to let him talk.

Her curiosity was answered when Carl immediately started to speak. "Amy, Amanda and I saw your presentation. It's obvious you are a first-rate detective, so we knew you would get in touch with me. You don't have to explain why you're here; I'll give you the play-by-play. I only started attending the Men's Discussion Group in late December. I enjoyed it a great deal. Max wasn't there for that meeting. The next time the group met, it was the first week in January. Max showed up and started calling people names. I couldn't believe this kind of disrespect was even allowed. When I said I believed we should limit immigration to people with skills that can benefit our country, he responded, 'You mean limit integration to European white people. You must be real close and cozy with the Klan.'

"At that point, I just snapped. I would have bashed his brains in if they hadn't stopped me from getting to him. I walked out of the room at that point. I went home and told Amanda what had transpired. She told me, in no uncertain terms, that violence was not an acceptable response, no matter what Max had said, and that I must avoid any future contact of any kind with Max. She said he was clearly poison.

"So I contacted Nicholas Razar, the coordinator for the group, and told him that as long as Max was in the group, I could not attend the meetings. He said he understood, and he was seriously considering trying to institute a policy where people who use insults will be suspended from being able to attend the group meetings. I asked him why such a policy hadn't always been in place. He said some people felt it could be abused by people claiming that views differing with their own constitute an insult, as is happening at a lot of colleges nowadays. After that, I followed Amanda's instructions; I totally avoided Max and never spoke to him again.

"Obviously, there was no justification for anyone to murder Max, no matter what he said to them. After my altercation with Max, I asked around, and I discovered that Max had insulted scores of residents of this community. So, Amy, you probably have more suspects in this murder case than in any other case you've ever investigated."

Amy laughed. "You sure as hell are right about that! Did you rejoin the Men's Discussion Group after Max was killed?"

"Yes, I did. And it is one of the highlights of each week for me."

"Where were you on the afternoon of the murder?"

Now Amanda chimed in. "He was with me all afternoon. We were home together until two. Then we went to the club event at the social hall. We walked around together for about an hour, and then we went back home together."

"Did you two speak to anyone in particular when you were in the social hall?"

Again, Amanda responded. "At this point, I don't remember any specifics. Honey, do you?"

Carl shook his head. "No, dear, I don't remember any specifics either."

Amy departed and went back to the hotel. She arrived at eleven thirty and found her husband with a big smile on his face. "Sweetheart, about a half hour ago, I wrapped up the computer work I had to do for my client!"

"You must be very relieved."

"That's an understatement."

Amy checked the phone records the deputy sheriff had sent, as well as the Men's Discussion Group attendance sheets. Then she reviewed the two morning interviews with her husband.

"Jerry, I just checked the records. They do show a call from Wendell's phone to Max's phone on the day after the meeting where the two had their blow-up. So Wendell was telling me the truth about phoning Max. I cannot determine whether he apologized to Max during that call, but that would be the logical reason why the call would be made."

Jeremy nodded. "Actually, I can't think of any other plausible reason for the call. I think you can eliminate Wendell as a suspect. On the other hand, just like with Ray, having Carl's wife come in and say they were together the whole time is extremely suspicious."

"Yeah, I'm pretty sure Wendell didn't do it. And for sure, Ray and Carl are still on my list. But I guess we'll have to put all this aside for the next few hours. We have to concentrate on Pete Sandover, my father's friend. Let's hope that whatever his problem is, our participation can be over in a very short period of time, because after today, we only have four more days left to investigate Max's murder."

Jeremy played party pooper. "Do you really have any hope of solving this case? There's no physical evidence to help you out. You've basically interviewed all the obvious suspects. They have their stories, and they're sticking to them. You have only four days left. It looks pretty bleak."

"Jerry, I should have interviewed every member of the YMC, as well as more members of the Men's Discussion Group, but I just don't have the time. In any case, I won't deny the obvious. My solving this murder has always been a long shot. Everyone here knows that. I'm giving it the old college try. I'm going to do some serious thinking and narrow my suspects down to the two or three most likely killers. Then I'll go back and interview those suspects a second time. Maybe they'll say something incriminating, or maybe I can trip them up in some way. If not, so be it."

"Assuming we can't wrap things up quickly with regard to Pete, it has to be up to you to decide if and when we should bow out. This man is your father's friend, so it has to be your call."

Amy nodded. "Agreed."

Friday, March 27, 2015, p.m.

At one twenty-five, Carole Bell opened her front door and told Amy and Jeremy to proceed to the living room. She said she'd join them there in two minutes. Jeremy observed the balding back of Irving's head as he relaxed on a chair in the living room, watching MSNBC. He decided to have a little political fun with his father-in-law.

"Irving, why don't you turn to Fox News Channel, so you can get some real news coverage, rather than pure left-wing propaganda?"

But when the target of his taunt turned to face him, Jeremy received a surprise. "Sorry, but I'm not Irving; I'm Pete Sandover. Irving is in the powder room." Amy burst out laughing.

Jeremy turned red. "I'm so embarrassed. But the back of your head has the same bald spot as Irving's, and your hair color is the same."

Pete turned off the TV. "Hey, no harm, no foul. Thank you so much—both of you—for coming and agreeing to hear about my situation."

At this point, Irving and Carole arrived at the living room, and everyone took seats. Irving asked Pete to tell Amy and Jeremy about his problem. Pete nodded and began.

"Well, it's not necessarily a problem. It could actually be a fantastic money-making opportunity for me. It started seven weeks ago tomorrow. I received an email from an organization named STTA, which stands for Short-Term Trend Analysis. They said that they were providing me with a free five-week trial subscription to their service.

"Every weekend, STTA selects the thirty most highly volatile stocks from the past week. However, they only consider stocks that have high trading volume. They plug those thirty stocks into their proprietary computer algorithm. The algorithm mainly uses technical chart analysis, although it also uses other inputs, and it spits out the one stock out of those thirty which is overwhelmingly likely to rise—or fall—during the following week. They send that stock out to their subscribers, plus either the word 'rise' or the word 'fall.' They don't say by how much the stock will rise or fall. But that's why they stick to the thirty most volatile stocks. These stocks will move several points—either up or down—during most weeks.

"Now here's what happened. For five weeks in a row, the stock they sent me did what they said it would do. For two of the five weeks, they said the stock they sent me would rise, and it did. For the other three weeks, they said the stock they sent me would fall, and it did.

"You have to understand that if an investor knows that a stock will rise a few points in the coming week, that investor can make a nice profit by buying the stock at the opening price on Monday and selling at the closing price on Friday. Even more money might be made if the investor buys on margin or buys calls on the stock. A similar profit can be made by selling short or buying puts, if the investor knows the stock is going to fall.

"Of course, I was not acting on these recommendations, but I did compute what I would have earned as profit if I had invested the funds which I had available to me. My average weekly earnings would have been three thousand nine hundred dollars. In the worst week, I would have earned sixteen hundred dollars. In the best week, seven thousand one hundred dollars."

Amy interrupted. "What if they said a stock will go up, but the opening price on Monday is much higher than the closing price the previous Friday?"

Pete nodded. "Good question. They said we should put in our Monday morning buy orders, prior to the market opening, at a limit price of half a point above the Friday closing price. If the stock never got down to that level on Monday, then the recommendation would be cancelled, and we should wait for the next week's recommendation. There was a similar rule if they said the stock would go down. But those scenarios never actually arose.

"Anyhow, on the Saturday after week five, I received an email from STTA which noted that they had been correct for five weeks in a row. It offered me the next week's stock for a special discount price of two hundred dollars. I sent them the money. They sent me the stock, and I acted on their recommendation. They were right again. I earned two thousand seven hundred dollars, and that's after subtracting the two hundred I paid them.

"On the next Saturday—this past Saturday—they requested one thousand dollars for their next pick. I got cold feet. I replied that their price was too high. They responded that it would not be fair to charge me less than their other clients, but they'd get back to me the next Saturday—which is tomorrow—to see if I had a change of heart. They said the one thousand dollar figure is their standard, constant price from now on. They won't raise it in future weeks, nor will they lower it.

"As I see it, I have three choices. Choice one is that I stop now and decline to ever pay the one thousand dollars. This ends my relationship with STTA. Choice two is that I send them the one thousand dollars and keep paying the thousand dollars per week as long as I am happy with the results. Obviously they can't be perfect forever, but even if they are wrong three or four times per year, I could earn more with them annually than my annual salary for most years when I was working.

"Then there is choice three. I can speak to some other SDE residents that I know are investors. I can tell them what I've just told you and ask if they want to join me. The more people we get, the less each of us has to put up. STTA will never find out that I'm sharing their stock with the other residents. Theoretically, if I can find ninety-nine other investors—of course that's more than I'd ever get—we would only have to put up ten dollars each per week.

"However, I know what the disadvantage is of choice three, and it's a big one. If the other investors lose money, they'll blame me. I want good relations with everyone in this community. It may not be worth it, even if it is by far the most financially beneficial choice. So, Amy, Jeremy, that's where I am."

Irving laughed. "Pete, whatever you do, don't ask me to get involved. Wall Street is a totally corrupt bunch of crooks. It was set up to make the rich richer. The brokerage firms slowly transfer their clients' money to themselves.

"I'll tell you a joke that illustrates my point. An investor complains to his broker that he followed the broker's investment advice and lost a lot of money. The broker says, 'Hey, I made money and my firm made money. Two out of three isn't bad'!"

Amy and Jeremy burst out laughing. Carole and Pete had clearly heard Irving tell the joke before.

Pete smiled. "Irving, the thought of asking you to participate never even came close to entering my mind."

But Irving wasn't finished. "I've got one more joke for you. It's even better, but it's a little long. A new client comes in and asks the broker assigned to him what stock he should buy. The broker says, 'I have a hot one, Big Win Industries. Today, you'll have to pay three bucks a share for it. By next Monday, you'll have to pay five bucks.' The new client buys a thousand shares.

"The client calls the broker the next Monday. 'How's Big Win?' The broker says, 'Like I told you, now you've got to pay five bucks a share. And next Monday, I'm confident it'll cost you nine bucks a share.' The client buys another eight hundred shares.

"This goes on for several additional weeks, with the stock price rising and the client continuing to buy. On the following Monday, the client comes into the office and the broker says, 'As I predicted last week, now you'll have to pay thirty dollars a share if you want to buy more Big Win.' The client announces, 'I'm satisfied with my profit on this stock, so sell everything.' The broker has a confused look on his face. 'Sell? To whom?' he asks."

Now the whole room was in hysterics, with Irving himself laughing the hardest. Eventually, they all calmed down, and Pete turned back to Amy, who put down her iPhone and spoke.

"I've been on the Web, trying to see if there's anything there regarding STTA or Short-Term Trend Analysis. I'm finding nothing whatsoever about them. That doesn't mean they don't have a successful computer algorithm, but it's a red flag. Jerry, what's the probability that if the rise-versus-fall predictions were made at random, they would be right six weeks in a row?"

"Well, there's always a small chance that the selected stock would be unchanged for the week, which would foul things up. But putting that aside, the probability would be one out of sixty-four."

Amy nodded. "So it looks to me like these guys do indeed have a good computer algorithm. How good, I can't tell you, but I doubt that they were just lucky. Maybe skill, plus a little luck."

Jeremy saw where Amy might be heading and decided it was time for him to take over. "Sweetheart, I am ninety-nine percent sure that I know exactly what's going on here. And I will—to use the phrase you use when you explain to me how you've solved a case—lay it all out for everyone.

"Pete, first, and most important, be sure never to send them any more money. Flag their emails as junk. And do not tell anyone about these people. You should be thrilled that due to sheer luck, you ended up ahead twenty-seven hundred dollars."

Pete was confused. "You're saying that STTA actually hit a lucky winning streak which had a probability of one out of sixty-four?"

Jeremy smiled. "No, this was a much better scam than just relying on a lucky streak. There are ways that people can get lists of email addresses—both legally, from reputable sources, and illegally, from hackers. STTA procured such a list. Maybe they succeeded in getting an email address list of people who had requested to receive financial information via email. That would be the best kind of list for them. But one way or another, they got a list of, let's say, sixty-four hundred email addresses. It could have been more; it could have been less. But using the number sixty-four hundred makes things work out nicely for me.

"Let's start with week one: They select a stock. Then they will divide their sixty-four hundred email addresses into two groups of thirty-two hundred each. For the first group, they send out emails predicting that their selected stock will rise. For the second group, they predict that their stock will fall. Obviously they will be correct for one group or the other—remember that we are disregarding the possibility that the stock will be unchanged.

"Now they discard the email addresses to which they sent the wrong prediction. We arrive at week two. For the thirty-two hundred remaining addresses, they again divide them into two groups. They select a new stock and send out sixteen hundred emails saying this new stock will rise, and sixteen hundred emails saying the stock will fall. Again, they discard the group of emails which receive the wrong prediction.

"So week three begins with sixteen hundred email addresses, to which they have already sent two correct predictions. Using the same process, that week ends with eight hundred addresses receiving three correct predictions. After week four, there will be four hundred addresses having four correct predictions. And after week five, two hundred people will be delighted to observe that they have received five correct predictions in a row. They will conclude that STTA has an amazingly successful predictive algorithm! They will be offered a week-six stock prediction, for the bargain price of only two hundred dollars.

"Obviously, a certain fraction of those two hundred individuals— the fraction will be small or large, depending on the quality of the list that STTA acquired—will be either uninterested in speculating in stocks, or financially unable to do so. Let's assume that only twenty-five percent decide to accept the offer. That's fifty people who send in two hundred dollars each, making ten thousand dollars. STTA doesn't care if those people convince friends to come in on the deal; it doesn't affect their income.

"For week six, STTA selects a stock and sends twenty-five emails saying it will rise and twenty-five saying it will fall. So half of the fifty remaining investors will have a horrible letdown. They will lose money on the stock, as well as losing their two hundred dollar payment to STTA. Disenchanted, they will vow never to be fooled again.

"But twenty-five investors will be thrilled to have made a nice profit and anxious to continue their relationship with STTA, which now requires one thousand dollars per week. Maybe ten investors will drop out at this point. But fifteen investors will continue, so STTA will pocket an additional fifteen thousand dollars.

"They will continue in this way for a number of weeks, until the point where there are no investors remaining who are willing to pay. They will probably take in a grand total of around forty thousand dollars—possibly a good deal more. Then, a few weeks later, they will acquire another list of email addresses, change their name, and run the scam again.

"Pete, you were one of the two hundred people who happened to receive five straight correct predictions. Then you put up the two hundred dollars for week six. Whichever prediction they gave you—rise or fall—had a fifty-fifty chance to be correct. You lucked out."

Amy gave Jeremy a big hug. "Oh my God! Now that you explain the whole thing, it's so obvious. Jerry, you are a genius! Now you all know why I married him."

Jeremy was self-effacing. "I don't deserve that much credit. As an actuary, I'm heavily into probability and numbers in general, so I was able to realize what was happening."

Pete chimed in, "Thank you so much, Jeremy. You probably saved me from losing money and from possibly alienating my friends. You and Amy are now my heroes."

Carole smiled and said, "Irving, aren't you now embarrassed and ashamed of all those unpleasant things you said to Jeremy regarding politics?"

"Absolutely not!" Irving exclaimed, and everyone laughed.

"Amy, Jeremy," said Pete, "may I have the pleasure of taking you two out to dinner this coming Sunday evening, at the restaurant of your choice?"

Amy nodded. "Pete, we would love that. I know where we'd like to go, if it's all right with you: Ruth's Chris Steak House in Phoenix. And if they are available, I'd like Mom and Dad to come too."

"No problem," said Pete. "Irving, Carole, can you come?" They immediately agreed.

"Now, everyone," said Amy, "Jerry and I have to leave and get back to working on the murder of Max Gattner."

It took them ten more minutes before they actually were able to depart, and they drove back to the hotel. At three fifteen, as they entered their room, Amy told Jeremy she was frustrated.

"Something bothered me that came up while we were at my parents' house. I told myself that I should think more about it, but I was immediately distracted, and now I cannot remember what it was."

"Did it have some connection to Max's murder?"

"It could have; I'm not sure what it may have been connected to. I'm sure I'll eventually think of it, but at this point, I'm a bit agitated. I know what'll make me feel better: I'll call Denise and tell her how smart you are. I'll bet she can't figure out the scam." Amy punched in the number.

Denise answered, and Amy told her they were on speakerphone. Amy commenced to rave on about her husband the genius. She then challenged Denise to solve Pete's problem. Amy had gone about 20 percent of the way through the presentation when Denise interrupted her.

"You don't have to go on any further. This is almost surely the scam where they send half the people a recommendation in one direction and send the other half a recommendation in the opposite direction. There are two books for investors, which I've read, which discuss this. One of the authors calls it the fifty-fifty scam."

"Denise, I hate you!" shouted Amy into the phone. Denise burst out laughing, as Amy continued to rant. "How can you know everything? Stop reading all those books!"

"Amy, you wouldn't want me to stop reading, any more than I would want you to be less brilliant as a detective."

"That's true, but right now, I still hate you! Denise, you are the most amazing woman I have ever met. I have said this since shortly after I met you."

"That didn't stop you from investigating me and finding out my secrets."

"You have a point. But you know I had to do that."

"Yes, I know. And Amy, you know how much I admire and respect you. You have incredible talents that no one else has."

Jeremy had heard all he could take. He spoke loudly, so Denise could hear. "This mutual admiration society has gone far enough. I get it: You two like each other!" Everyone laughed, and Amy got off the phone.

Jeremy kissed his wife. "Sweetheart, how much of a genius can I be when I've seen Irving many times, and I still couldn't tell the difference between him and Pete? I was so embarrassed!"

Amy exploded. "Oh my God, that's it! That's what I was trying to remember! Oh my God; I've got to think! I've got to think!" She ran into the bathroom and shut the door. After a minute of silence, Jeremy heard screams coming from inside the bathroom.

"Oh my God! Oh my God!" Amy opened the door, ran out, and started kissing her husband all over his face, still shouting. "You solved the case! You solved the case! You solved the case!" Jeremy began to laugh.

"No, Jerry, I'm not joking." Amy started to calm down a bit. "*You* actually solved the case. I can't prove anything, but you solved the case."

"Sorry, sweetheart; I wasn't laughing because I thought you were joking. I was laughing because when you shouted 'You solved the case! You solved the case!' it reminded me of Russ Hodges shouting, 'The Giants win the pennant! The Giants win the pennant'!"

Amy was dumbfounded. "What?"

"It's a famous line from baseball; he shouted that on the radio after Bobby Thomson's big home run. But I don't see how anything I said could have solved the case."

"I'll explain it all to you in due time. But you were also right about your two big general questions regarding this murder case—questions for which we couldn't come up with satisfactory answers—particularly the first one, about the time gap. My solution answers both questions perfectly. Now that what you said has given me the solution, it's so obvious that we should have thought of it a long time ago. But of course nobody realized it, until I just did."

"But you say you have no proof?"

Amy nodded. "Right. I have no proof whatsoever. But I'm nearly one hundred percent certain that I am correct. I know who killed Max. My solution makes everything fit perfectly. Now, I have to call Ralph." Amy punched in the number.

"Hi, Ralph, it's Amy. I have a question for you."

"Okay, shoot."

"On the afternoon of Max's murder, how much total time did you spend in club room B when you brought the caps in? Please include the time you spent in the adjoining men's room."

"Let's see. I was in the club room for between thirty and forty-five seconds. I said hello to Max, and I told him I was bringing in the new caps that the YMC had ordered. He told me to leave the box next to his chair, as he was going to select a cap for himself. I told him I'd be returning to the club room in time for the movie. Then I went into the men's room. I spent less than a minute there. Okay, I'll admit it: I'm pretty sure I didn't wash my hands."

Amy laughed at this revelation—she was trying not to, but she couldn't control herself. "Sorry, but men don't often admit that. I appreciate your candor. So, based on what you say, the total time was roughly a minute and a half, right?"

"Right. Why is this important?"

"I hope, at some point, to be able to answer that question for you, but if I do, it will not be today."

"That's very mysterious! But I guess that's all you're going to tell me."

"Regretfully, yes. By the way, when you were in the men's room, do you recall whether you were alone there?"

"I believe I was alone, but I'm not sure."

Amy thanked Ralph, got off the phone, and called Mel Barton.

"Hello, Amy. How's your investigation going?"

"Well, I'm still doing interviews. I want to cover as many bases as I can. I'm going to speak to Christine Harwood. I understand that your wife, Annette, is a friend of hers. I hear they go shopping together."

"Yes, they're good friends."

"Can you put Annette on the phone?"

"Sure."

At this point, Amy put on the speakerphone. After a few seconds, Annette came on. "Hello, Amy. I was with Mel at your presentation. I guess we've made a lot of trouble for you."

"As I told Mel, I'm glad you did. I'm in the process of interviewing people who have or have had leadership roles in the community. I understand that Christine Harwood has served as chairperson of the activities committee. I plan to interview Christine, and, as you are her friend, I would like you to tell me a little bit about Christine."

"Okay, Christine is a very enthusiastic person. She likes to be a leader. She relished her time as chair of the activities committee, and she hopes that Darren is healthy enough to run for board president next year. She thinks Darren has a decent chance to win, and then she will be back as activities chair."

"I presume," chimed in Amy, "that Christine serves on several committees."

"Yes, but she has told me that she is often frustrated that people on the committees where she serves don't give sufficient consideration to the ideas she presents. When she was chair of the activities committee, she was the big kahuna. Now she's a nobody, and it's much less satisfying for her."

"Annette, I know people like that. They are unfulfilled if they can't lead. Christine was probably an important executive when she was in the business world."

"Yes, she was a pretty high-level manager, and she supervised many employees."

"I also heard that Christine is an athlete—she's an excellent volleyball player. I understand she plays every Saturday morning."

"Well, she's big on volleyball and a talented player. She loves the Saturday games; I play in those games too, but I'm not at her skill level."

"Yes," Amy recalled, "when I came to see Mel last Saturday morning, you told me you were leaving to play volleyball."

"You have a good memory. Interesting that you mentioned Saturday volleyball. Christine almost never misses the weekly games, but she has missed the last two Saturdays. And she told me she won't be playing volleyball tomorrow."

"Did Christine tell you why she was missing the volleyball?"

"All she would tell me was that she had to schedule some appointments in Phoenix, and the only availability is on Saturdays at ten in the morning."

"Sounds like she's seeing a doctor."

"That's what I've been thinking. She's been complaining of headaches in recent weeks. Also, she has been nauseated and vomiting. So I hope she's getting the appropriate medical care."

"Annette, can you get me Christine's cell phone number?"

"Sure." Amy took down the number, thanked Annette, and hung up. Then she phoned the number Annette had given her. "Hello, Christine, this is Amy Bell."

"Hi, Amy. Sorry I missed your presentation, and I also missed you when you came to talk to Darren."

"That's why I called. I'm trying to interview all residents who have or have had leadership positions, so I would like to speak to you. Can we meet tomorrow afternoon?"

"Sure. Can you be here at three o'clock?"

"No problem, I'll see you then."

Amy got off the phone, and Jeremy had a question. "Did Christine Harwood have any interaction with Max?"

"Well, Darren was board president, and Max was being a jerk at the public board meetings. I presume that Christine was also in attendance. At that time, she was also activities committee chair, and she could have had some run-ins with Max in that role."

"But sweetheart, that was several years ago. Did you find out about any blow-ups between Max and Christine—or even between Max and Darren—during the weeks before Max's death?"

"No, I would guess there weren't any recent blow-ups. If there were, Darren would most likely have told me about them when I interviewed him. Darren and Max were both members of the YMC, so they did interact a bit. But I have no reason to believe there was any recent interaction whatsoever between Max and Christine."

"So, why are you interviewing Christine tomorrow afternoon, and why are you asking Annette so many questions about her?"

Amy rose from her chair, walked over to where her husband was sitting and began to stroke him on the cheek. "Poor, poor boy! Don't you know the answer to that question?"

"No, of course I don't know."

Amy stopped the stroking and stood in front of her husband, with a smile on her face. "Jerry, the reason I'm asking questions about Christine, and the reason I want to interview her tomorrow is that Christine murdered Max!"

Jeremy was incredulous. "What?"

"She killed Max, and you solved the case for me."

"For God's sake, that's crazy. You said they hadn't interacted. Why would she want to kill Max?"

Amy now resumed the stroking of Jeremy's cheek. "Poor, poor boy. You ask me why Christine would want to kill Max. The answer is that Christine did not want to kill Max. She didn't want to harm Max at all!"

Jeremy now had it all figured out. "Okay, sweetheart, I get it. This is a big put-on. It's like what your brothers did to me last Sunday at the big affair. Soon, you're gonna say 'gotcha!' and tell me who really did it. And you probably just want to ask Christine a question regarding someone else, probably regarding the real killer."

Amy continued stroking. "I'm not playing a trick on you. Christine murdered Max, but she had no intention of killing him. When she swung that bat down on her victim's head, she thought she was killing Ralph Blackstone. Let's cuddle together on the couch, and I'll lay it all out for you."

"See, sweetheart, that's what I told everyone you always say!" They got comfortable on the couch and Amy began.

"Darren and Christine Harwood had achieved important leadership positions in the community, which they had coveted since they had arrived. Darren was board president, and Christine was activities chair. Then, in February 2012, along came Ralph, who spoiled it for both of them, particularly for Christine. Darren didn't care as much about losing his position as Christine did about losing hers. She was devastated. She prevailed on Darren to run again for board president, in 2013 and 2014, but Ralph kept beating him, although the vote was getting closer. Christine hated Ralph for ruining everything.

"She got Darren to run again in 2015 and thought her husband had a decent chance to win. Darren knew how badly his wife wanted the activities chair, and he pushed himself too hard in his election campaigning. He suffered a heart attack. Christine blamed Ralph for causing her husband to almost die.

"Two days after Darren's heart attack, the clubhouse had the club event in the social hall. That morning, Christine had visited her husband at the hospital. We know that after she got back home, she went to the clubhouse, because Darren told me Christine called him from the clubhouse café at two fifteen to give him the latest gossip.

"Sometime between five and ten past three, Christine was in the hall and saw Ralph enter club room B. He was wearing a YMC jacket and a Mets cap. He was carrying a box of caps. Her husband's heart attack, two days earlier, had greatly amplified the hatred Christine already felt toward Ralph. As Darren was a member of the YMC, she knew about the Yogi Berra bat, conveniently located on a table in the back of the club room.

"At this point, there are two possible scenarios, but I think the first scenario is less likely. Christine thought about it for a couple of minutes or just waited until there was no one else in the hall, and then she decided to act. She took a pair of gloves out of her handbag and put them on. Or maybe she took out a scarf. She planned to quietly enter the club room and, if Ralph was alone, she would attempt to kill him with the bat. She entered and saw there was only one person in the room, sitting on a chair with his back to the door. This man was wearing a YMC jacket and a Mets hat. The box she had seen Ralph carrying into the room was sitting right next to this man's chair. Of course this man was Ralph; Christine never even dreamed of any other possibility. She quietly grabbed the bat, came up behind the man, and bashed him on the head three times. Then she dropped the bat and quickly exited the room unobserved, maybe via the ladies' room.

"Actually, in the brief period prior to Christine entering the room in an attempt to kill Ralph, her victim had left the premises. Ralph exited via the men's room to a hall around the corner from where Christine was standing, so she didn't observe him leaving. Christine may not have realized that she had killed Max until sometime later. You can imagine her shock when she found out.

"By the way, Max was five foot nine, and Ralph is roughly the same height. So Max's general size while sitting, when viewed from behind, would be similar to Ralph's—not that Christine would be that observant. And Christine is an athletic woman—she's an excellent volleyball player—so she'd have had no problem swinging the bat down onto Max's head.

"There is a second scenario, which I believe is more likely, particularly due to the pen found under the table. After a couple of minutes, Christine decided to go into the club room and have it out verbally with Ralph. She was going to accuse him of causing her husband to have a heart attack. She would say that if he had any decency, he would drop out of the race now, or at least not run for reelection in 2016, which would then allow Darren to become board president without a tough campaign that could cause him to have another heart attack and probably kill him. But when she entered the room and saw the man she assumed was Ralph sitting on the chair, oblivious to her presence, she realized that this was her big chance. She could kill Ralph, and thereby open the door for her and her husband to regain their leadership positions, while at the same time getting rid of someone she hated for knocking them off their pedestals at SDE and for causing Darren to have a heart attack. She took the gloves or scarf out of her handbag—probably dropping a pen in the process—grabbed the bat, and bashed the man on the head.

"Of course, in both scenarios, I assume that Christine got rid of the gloves or scarf. I presume she has not told Darren what she did. He impressed me as a really nice guy, who would be horrified—and that's an understatement—if he ever found out what his wife did.

"And Jerry, if you hadn't looked at the back of Pete's head and mistaken him for my father, I'm pretty sure I never would have solved the case. So you essentially solved two cases in one day!"

Jeremy smiled and nodded. "Sweetheart, you are incredible! It's obvious to me that your solution is almost certainly correct. And Denise was right; no one else would have solved this case. I also see how your solution answers the two big questions. First, there was no big time gap, because Christine committed the murder only a couple of minutes after she saw Ralph enter the club room. And second, the event that caused the killer to reach a critical mass of rage occurred only two days prior to the murder."

"Yep, the two big questions are answered. So now, I'm sure you know what we're gonna do tomorrow morning."

He took a guess. "Are we going to figure out some questions for you to ask—when you interview Christine—that might get her to trip up and incriminate herself? That would seem to be the only way we can prove she did it."

Amy nodded. "I think you're right to say that's the only way to get any proof. I doubt she'll give herself away, but I can hope. By the way, I plan to bring a mini recording device—I don't know why I brought it to Arizona, but I'm glad I did. And I do have to figure out what I'm gonna ask Christine in the interview. But that's not what we're doing tomorrow morning. We're going to get up early, park near Christine's house, and follow her when she drives out, so we can see where she's going that causes her to miss her volleyball games."

Jeremy feared the worst. "What time do we have to get up?"

"We'll get up at six fifteen and leave here at seven thirty. We'll probably have to wait at least an hour near the Harwoods' house, but we can't take a chance. So we'll be going to bed tonight at around ten. And at six fifteen this evening, we'll go out to Barini's for dinner."

Amy was clearly not requesting Jeremy's approval with regard to any of these decisions. When she was on a roll like this, he realized that it was useless to protest or suggest any revisions.

And Amy was not finished giving orders. "So that leaves the time between now and six fifteen." Amy gave her husband a look that could only mean one thing. "You may be a big, smart man—actually a genius, in probability at least—but I'm taking you down! Take your clothes off, get two pillows from the bed, and get on the rug—now! I want you flat on your back and naked." Jeremy could sense part of him getting larger, and he understood that the conversation was over.

Saturday, March 28, 2015, a.m.

At 8:55 a.m., Amy and Jeremy had been sitting in their car for over an hour. They were parked on Red Rock Drive, a few doors down from the Harwoods' home. Jeremy had spent the time daydreaming about the fantastic veal parmesan he had enjoyed for dinner at Barini's, as well as about Amy having taken him down prior to their going out for the meal. But now he saw the Harwoods' garage door open. "Sweetheart, she's leaving."

Amy watched the car pull out. She turned on her ignition to follow. "Look, Jerry—Darren is with her. If they're going to a doctor, it must be pretty serious."

Forty-five minutes later, the Harwoods arrived at the parking lot of the North Phoenix Cancer Center. Amy parked her car a distance away from them. She observed Darren and Christine holding hands as they walked to the entrance and went in.

"Jerry, we'll have to wait here for about forty-five minutes; then we'll go in and see if we can determine the name of the doctor she's seeing."

"Amy, I've got to use the men's room; I don't know if I can wait that long."

"We can't go in while they might be there in the waiting room, which could be right near the entrance. Darren would recognize me, and he's probably seen you with me at the clubhouse or elsewhere around the community. I should have thought to have us bring disguises to put on."

At ten fifteen, Jeremy said he couldn't wait any longer, so Amy agreed to take a chance. They went into the building. Luckily, the Harwoods were not around when Amy walked up to the reception desk and checked the patient sign-in sheets. There were apparently only three doctors seeing patients on this Saturday morning. Christine's name was written on the sheet for Dr. Sanford Wallop. It had a line through it, to indicate that she had already gone in to see the doctor.

Taking a cue from her husband, Amy also visited the restroom; then she and Jeremy returned to their car. Amy got on the Internet, using her iPhone. It didn't take her long to get the information she was seeking. "Dr. Sanford Wallop specializes in brain tumors. He is described as one of the top doctors in the country in that field. He only has appointments with patients in Phoenix on Saturday mornings; on the other days he works out of Green Valley, which is south of Tucson."

"Sweetheart, don't some people with brain tumors start to act violently on occasion?"

Amy briefly did some more research. "Yes, some do. Also, some common symptoms are headaches, nausea, and vomiting, which is what Annette said was happening to Christine."

"I don't want to sound morbid, but if the brain tumor is bad enough, Christine won't live long enough for you to have to worry about finding proof she killed Max."

Amy nodded. "Yes, some brain tumors are inoperable and fast-growing. But most can be treated in some way, and the individual could live a long time."

At ten after eleven, they saw Christine and Darren emerge from the cancer center, again holding hands, as they proceeded to their car and drove off. Amy again followed them in her car, as they returned to their South Desert Estates home. At this point, Amy drove back to the hotel with her husband.

"Sweetheart, how does this affect the way you will conduct your interview?" asked Jeremy as they entered their room.

"I'm not sure how to handle the interview, but I now think it's overwhelmingly likely that Darren will be present with his wife when I speak with her. That may be a disadvantage for me. And I'm gonna ask her if she has a pen I can borrow. I want to see if she keeps a pen in her handbag, hopefully a Bic Soft Feel retractable.

"I know we're very confident that the case is solved. But still, I'd still like to see some physical confirmation that I'm right. The pen wouldn't prove anything, but it makes sense that when she was standing next to the table with the bat on it, a pen could have fallen out of her handbag while she was taking out her scarf or gloves."

Jeremy nodded. "Yeah, it makes sense. If Christine has that Bic pen in her bag, it would be icing on the cake, even though we know it's a common pen around here. Of course, as you said, the only way to get proof is to get her to slip up."

"I know, and I'm not looking forward to what I have to do."

Saturday, March 28, 2015, p.m.

At one twenty, Amy's phone rang. It was Annette Barton. "Hi, Amy, I just wanted to let you know that I heard from Christine. She said she's hoping to be able to play volleyball with us next Saturday morning; she won't be going to that appointment that she's had for the past three Saturdays. Maybe she was seeing a doctor and got the treatment she needed."

"I hope so. Did Christine tell you she went to see a doctor?"

"No, and when she called, I asked her what the Saturday appointments were all about, but she changed the subject."

Amy thanked Annette for calling and got off the phone. "Jerry, I don't know whether what Annette said is good news or bad news, with regard to Christine's tumor. She's not going back to see Dr. Wallop next Saturday. She told Annette she'll try to play volleyball. That could mean he told her there's nothing more they can do at this point. Or maybe he's sending her somewhere else for treatment and doesn't have to see her every week from now on."

"Sweetheart, why don't you just phone Dr. Wallop and ask him?" They both laughed.

"Jerry, if only the detective business were that easy!"

Before heading to Red Rock Drive, Amy drove to the SDE club-house. There, she surreptitiously snatched a Bic Soft Feel retract-able pen from the reception desk and put it in her handbag.

At three minutes past three, Amy rang the doorbell; Christine Harwood opened the door and invited Amy to join her in the living room. She said Darren would be joining them in a minute or two. Christine was five foot seven and athletic looking, but her face was thin and pale. She tried to smile at her guest, but Amy could see that she was not happy. Amy knew that Christine was sixty-three years old, but felt she looked somewhat older. Of course, given Christine's health problems, Amy wasn't surprised. Amy declined an offer of a drink. She immediately asked the question.

"Christine, I just discovered my pen is not working; do you have one in your bag that I can borrow?"

Her hostess reached into her handbag and produced a Bic Soft Feel retractable pen. Amy smiled, accepted the pen, and wrote a few words on her notepad. Amy noted that the ink was black. Then she opened her handbag.

"Oh gee, I see that I have another pen in here, and it's the same kind of Bic as yours. Mine is nearly unused, so here, take mine." Amy handed Christine the pen. At this time, Darren entered the living room and sat down next to his wife, who was on the sofa.

Amy continued, in a soft, low voice. "You know, the sheriff's people picked up a pen, probably dropped by the killer, under the table where the bat was."

"Yes," said Darren, "Mel mentioned that a pen had been found. He didn't say it was found by the sheriff."

"Right," responded Amy, as she stared at Christine, "the sheriff didn't want it known that he had the pen. It was a Bic Soft Feel retractable, just like the one you and I have." Now it was time for Amy to lie. "The sheriff also didn't want it known that his people found DNA on the pen.

"People don't realize how often DNA can be found on common items which they use, such as pens." Amy was still staring at Christine and observed a look of sheer terror on her face.

"Obviously, the sheriff can't request DNA samples from every SDE resident. But if I identify the prime suspect, the sheriff will do the necessary checking and matching." Amy glanced at Darren. Now he had a look of terror.

"When I accepted this investigation, one reason I did so was because my father lives in this community and asked for my help. But another reason is that if the killer is not identified, people at SDE will always be suspicious of each other and wonder if the killer may strike again. They shouldn't have to live that way."

"Amy," Christine interrupted, with her voice trembling, "I presume you want to know about my interactions with Max. I haven't had any interactions with Max for several years. In fact, I don't recall even seeing him since the public board meeting this past September."

"Actually, I wasn't going to ask you about Max." Amy resumed her stare at Christine. "I would like you to tell me about how you feel about Ralph Blackstone. In a way, he was responsible for Darren's heart attack."

Christine burst into hysterics. "He nearly killed my husband. He wanted to kill him. Darren was going to win the election. I couldn't let him kill my husband. I had to try—"

"Honey, that's enough." Darren stepped in as soon as he could. He rose and stood between his wife and Amy. "Christine hasn't been well lately. She's not thinking clearly at this point. Honey, I want you to go to the bedroom and take a little nap. I'll take a walk outside with Amy. I want to tell her about my plans for my 2016 election campaign against Ralph."

Ten minutes later, with Christine in bed, Amy and Darren began to walk slowly along Red Rock Drive. "Amy, you were outed. This morning, the receptionist—I don't have to tell you the location— asked me if I knew the five-foot-four, thirtyish, attractive woman with long black hair who walked up to the reception desk, looked at the names on the patient sign-in sheets, and then walked away. I told her I knew who you were.

"I assumed right then and there that you knew everything. And now, with what you just said to Christine, it is one hundred percent obvious that you know everything. So confirm for me what you know."

"I know that Christine killed Max; she thought she was killing Ralph."

"Amy, my wife told me last night that she had killed Max. As you said, Christine mistook him for Ralph. Until she told me, I had no idea. If it weren't for you, I'm sure no one would have ever found out. I realize it wouldn't have been fair to the community, but I would have kept her secret. I'm her husband—do you understand?"

"Yes, Darren, I understand."

"Well, you obviously know Christine has a brain tumor, but let me tell you the whole story. She has glioblastoma, which is the most aggressive cancer. Unfortunately, it was asymptomatic for a long time. The tumor wasn't discovered until it had reached an enormous size. Its RPA class is six, which is the worst. It is inoperable, and Dr. Gallop told me that it would take a miracle for any treatment to allow her to survive for more than four months, at the outside. At this time, my wife does not want the residents in SDE to know about any of this.

"Christine's condition will deteriorate rapidly from this point on. She's going to try to play volleyball next Saturday. I hope she can, but soon she won't be able to. Within a month or two, she'll have substantial memory loss and require constant medical assistance. Then she'll die. This is the prognosis, barring a miracle."

"Oh my God!" Amy was holding back tears. "Oh my God!"

Darren actually was crying at this point. "I'm sure the tumor— though it hadn't yet been diagnosed—was responsible for Christine killing Max. Under normal conditions, it would have been impossible for her to commit an act of violence like that."

Amy nodded. "You could very well be right."

"This is what I hope you will agree to do. We'll go back into the house. Christine's nap will not last long, and then she will write out a confession that she killed Max, but was not herself, due to the brain tumor. She will not mention Ralph. She will say her husband never knew. We will give the confession to you. You will promise not to release her confession until after Christine has died. If, after four months, Christine is still alive—which, I am very sorry to say, is extremely unlikely—you will be free to release the confession."

Amy was contemplative for a few seconds. "Darren, what about Ralph; will he be safe?"

"Amy, you have my word that Ralph will be absolutely safe. When Christine killed Max, it was a perfect storm, for her mental state, just two days after my heart attack. In addition, last night I told her—and she now clearly understands—that Ralph and I are actually friends, and I would be in great pain if anything happened to him."

"Darren, I'll have to say something to the community leaders before my husband and I end our visit here. I will say I am very confident that the case will be completely solved before this coming August first. When I release the confession, I may decide to say I had just recently attained possession of it."

Darren nodded. "That's fine."

"Okay, Darren, we have a deal. You have my word that I will wait up to four months, if necessary."

Darren, still in tears, said, "Amy, may I hug you?"

"Of course." They hugged and returned to the house. Amy sat at the dining room table; Darren went to speak to Christine. Forty-five minutes later, Darren returned and gave a handwritten letter to Amy. She read it aloud:

March 28, 2015

> I, Christine Harwood, confess that on January 31, I killed Max Gattner, by striking him several times on the head with a baseball bat. I was not my true self at that time; I was being influenced by a very large brain tumor which had not yet been diagnosed. My husband, Darren, is totally unaware of what I did. I am so very sorry, and I pray that everyone will try to forgive me.

Amy noted that Christine Harwood's signature was below the confession.

"Darren, can I just see a birthday card or cancelled check, or anything you can show me with Christine's signature on it?"

"Of course. I understand you have to be sure." He showed Amy a Valentine's Day card. Amy noted the handwritten words, "Dear Darren, you are my everything. Love, Christine." The writing was clearly the same as in the confession. Darren also provided Amy with an envelope, into which she placed the folded confession sheet.

A few minutes later, Amy departed. Before returning to the hotel, she stopped at a FedEx store and made several copies of the confession. At five fifteen, she got back to the hotel room and hugged and kissed her husband. "Jerry, it's over. I have Christine's confession." Amy related the entire story of her visit to the Harwoods' home.

"Sweetheart, it's amazing how you always know what to say and how to act to get the desired result. I think it was your fib about DNA on the pen that pushed Christine—and also Darren—over the edge."

Amy nodded. "That certainly could be true. Anyhow, if things go as expected, the residents at SDE will learn that under the influence of a brain tumor, Christine killed a man that many of them hated. There will be no reference to Ralph; no one will ever know the truth. And Darren can say he never knew what she did—which he told me was true until yesterday, and I believe him."

Jeremy smiled. "It's the best possible result. Not that they should think that way, but lots of residents will say that what happened to Max served him right, and they'll excuse his killer as being mentally impaired. And, most importantly, there will be closure in the community, regarding the murder."

Amy nodded again. "Amen. What do you say we leave here on Monday and do a little sightseeing? I'll set up a mini itinerary for us."

Her husband smiled. "Well, if you can finish up by tomorrow, that sounds great! I presume you want to meet with some of the community leaders and explain things. And then we're going out to dinner tomorrow evening at Ruth's Chris, with your parents and Pete."

"Yeah, I'll set up a meeting for Sunday with Ralph and some of the others, and then we'll finish off our SDE visit in style with some great steak dinners."

Sunday, March 29, 2015

At 2:15 p.m., Amy and Jeremy were sitting in the board office at the SDE clubhouse. The door was locked. Also seated in the office were Ralph and Susan Blackstone, Mel Barton, Nicholas Razar, and Amy's father.

"Thank you, everyone, for coming," Amy began. "Jerry and I will be leaving tomorrow morning. We will do a few days of sightseeing, and then we will return to Manhattan. I want to update you on my investigation of the killing of Max Gattner.

"This is an extraordinary case. Max was widely disliked, and therefore there were a very large number of potential suspects. I spoke to many residents of the community, and their cooperation in my investigation proved to be crucial. Also, Jerry was of tremendous assistance to me." Amy kissed her husband. "I can tell you now that I have made great progress. I am extremely confident that the case will be completely solved, no later than this coming August first—maybe a lot sooner. I have definite reasons for saying this, but they must remain confidential.

"I know this sounds a bit mysterious, and it is not my intention to be unnecessarily secretive. But I cannot elaborate on what I have just told you. You trusted and respected me enough to request my assistance. I am asking you to continue to trust me, and to respect my judgment. I am requesting, if you are discussing my investigation with other residents, that you say only that I have told you I am making great progress and expect to solve the murder. Tell them that our returning to New York does not affect my commitment to solving this case.

"I do want to emphasize that I am now convinced, based on my investigation, that this killing was a one-time event. There will not be any additional violent actions by the person or persons involved in Max's killing. And that's just about all I can tell you at this time. And, Dad, please don't bring up the case with me at dinner tonight."

Irving broke into laughter, as did several other people in the room.

"Amy," Ralph said, "I'm sure I speak for all of us in saying we are so very grateful that you agreed to investigate the case. You have put in many hours on this case, which you could have spent sightseeing with Jeremy. And I don't think any of us thought you would succeed in solving the murder. If, as you suggest, you are on the verge of solving the case, then you have pulled off a major miracle. And thank you, Jeremy, too."

Amy and Jeremy shook hands with everyone in the room. Then they all exited the board office, and Amy and Jeremy went back to the hotel. At five forty-five, they left for their dinner at Ruth's Chris Steak House.

After enjoying main courses of filet mignon, Amy and Jeremy were given a surprise for dessert. A chocolate cake, ordered by Pete, was placed on the table, with the words, "Thank you so much, Amy and Jeremy!" written on it.

Irving had honored Amy's request and had not brought up the murder case. Instead, for a decent period of time during dinner, he had engaged in a good-humored political debate with Pete.

As they were finishing the cake, Pete left to use the restroom. Carole asked, "Amy, do you and Jeremy know where you're going for the next few days?"

"Yes, we'll leave early tomorrow morning and drive to Lake Powell for two nights. Then, early Wednesday morning, we'll drive back to Sky Harbor Airport and take a midday flight home."

"Well, call us when you get to Lake Powell, and also when you arrive back home. Your father told me what you said at the clubhouse meeting, and that you don't want to talk any more about the case. Can't you tell us something additional?"

Amy smiled broadly. "Yes, I can. Here goes: Mom, Dad, I love you both." Everyone laughed.

Wednesday, June 10, 2015

At three twenty in the afternoon, Amy was at her Spy4U office when the phone rang. "Hello Amy, this is Darren Harwood. Christine died early this morning. We will have the funeral on Sunday. Then, per Christine's long-standing preference, she will be cremated."

"Oh my God, I'm so sorry."

"I will send you an email confirming her death. Can you please wait until next Tuesday before releasing the information you have?"

"Of course I'll wait till Tuesday. Thank you for phoning me. And again, I'm so very sorry."

Amy got home at five fifteen and kissed her husband. "Jerry, I have some news. Darren called me; Christine died this morning. We agreed I'll wait until next Tuesday—after the funeral—to release her confession. So the Max Gattner murder case will truly be over."

Jeremy nodded. "I guess Dr. Wallop's dire prognosis turned out to be correct. And I presume it is still your intention not to reveal the true reason why Christine attacked Max with the bat."

Now Amy nodded. "That's correct. The SDE residents will assume that Max had verbally abused Christine—just like he had verbally abused so many other people—and that abuse, plus the effects of the brain tumor, caused her to murder him."

"Well, sweetheart, on the brighter side, you solved the case, and we still got to visit Lake Powell. Wasn't the Antelope Canyon fantastic?"

"It sure was! And there's some other news. Cathy and Eddie would like to go out this Saturday afternoon to a big NYPD event. Cathy's parents won't be able to help them out, so we'll get to babysit Aurora! I told Cathy we'll be there at twelve thirty. They should get back home before six." Jeremy did not look pleased to hear this news, but Amy knew just what to say.

"Will you please wipe that disgusted look off your face? This is going to be fun!"

THE END

About The Author

D avid Schwinger is retired, having spent his entire career teaching mathematics at City College, City University of New York. He now lives in Florida with his wife, Sherryl, whom he met when she was his student. In addition to writing Amy Bell mysteries, he composes music and plays Ping-Pong and pickleball. He and Sherryl have travelled to over 125 countries. His neighbors challenged him to write a murder mystery that takes place in an active adult community, and this book is the result.

Disclaimer

Although some named locations, such as City College, are real, all depictions of persons, events, and policies at any and all locations in this book are intended to be completely fictional.

Made in the USA
San Bernardino, CA
14 May 2017